UNAVOIDABLE FATES

Also by Alexandria Blaelock

SHORT STORY COLLECTIONS
The Histories of Hayward Hall
Lovelorn, Lovestruck and Love at First Sight
Common or Garden Variety Heroes
Case Files of the Wilkinson Detective Agency
Unavoidable Fates
Christmas Travesties
Five Faces of Felicia Clarke
Little Place Called Home
Security Directorate Dossiers v. 1.
Security Directorate Dossiers v. 2.

FICTION
That Love Nonsense
Taipan vs Brown
The Ghost and Ms Cox
Friends Like That
Weaving the Wildwood
Wolf vs Orb

MS BLAELOCK'S BOOKS
Stress Free Dinner Parties
Signature Wardrobe Planning
Holistic Personal Finance
Minimally Viable Housekeeping
Planning a Life Worth Living

PICTURE BOOKS
Australia Felix

SELECTED SHORT STORIES
Alma's Grace
Blood and Bloody Profanity
Cancelled by the Cartel
Dingo Hunting
Honoris Virilis Respectu
Mince Pie Mystery
Remains of Christmas

UNAVOIDABLE FATES

ALEXANDRIA BLAELOCK

BlueMere Books
MELBOURNE, AUSTRALIA

For permission requests, please contact enquiries@bluemerebooks.com.

Ordering Information:
Discounts are available on quantity purchases. For details, contact orders@bluemerebooks.com.

Unavoidable Fates/Alexandria Blaelock
hardback ISBN: 978-1-925749-80-9
paperback ISBN: 978-1-925749-81-6
digital ISBN: 978-1-925749-82-3

Book Layout © BookDesignTemplates.com
Cover Art © Warm_Tail licenced from Shutterstock.com

For Mariëlle,
because, well,
Fate!

Fate leads him who follows it,
and drags him who resist.

– PLUTARCH

CONTENTS

INTRODUCTION

have been fascinated by the Fates since I was a child.

My first glimpse of them was watching the Sunday Night Movie on TV.

When cable didn't exist, and that was still a thing.

It was in my Australian childhood home, with the matching dark green and orange floral carpet and curtains - who does that these days?

And the burgundy three-piece lounge suite that came from England with us. A rocking arm chair each for Mum and Dad, and a three-seater couch nominally for me and my brother, though we were lying on the floor inches from the wood encased television screen.

Convenient when Mum or Dad wanted to change the channels, because remotes didn't exist in those days either.

A fire was blazing in the open fire place, which puts it sometime between 1973 and 1979.

I think the movie was a Ray Harryhausen film, mainly because it used "Dynamation," the stop motion photography technique he pioneered.

And I'm pretty sure it was one of the ones with skeleton warriors, but I've never checked.

Anyhow, Atropos brandished an enormous pair of scissors and cut some guy's thread.

Or at least that's how I remember it, who knows exactly how it was, (except someone who remembers that movie better than me).

I remember, the guy seemed pretty worried about it, and I was impressed by her power. Though at the time, I didn't understand what it was she had.

Sometimes I think I'd like to track down the movie and watch it again, but seeing it again would probably reduce her mystique for me.

The Fates are sister deities, incarnations of life and destiny, who control of fates of gods and mortals. In the Greek mythology they are known as the *Moirai*, and their names are:

- Clotho (the Spinner) who makes the thread. She's generally represented wearing red, and carrying a spindle and distaff. Or in more modern works, the Book of Life.
- Lachesis (the Alotter) who measures the thread. She dresses in black and carries a measuring staff.
- Atropos (the Inflexible) who determines the method of death and cuts the thread. She wears white and carries the shears. (As I said, enormous shears).

The fates also appear as the *Parcae* in Roman mythology, and there are corresponding myths of female destiny controlling deities in both Europe *and* Asia.

In some traditions, they merged to become a triple goddess who shows only one face at any given time. In this context, Clotho is the maiden, Lachesis the mother, and Atropos the crone.

Or more literally, the past, the present, and the future.

In 2011, I watched a hilarious New Zealand fantasy show called *The Almighty Johnsons*, featuring Norse gods incarnating in Auckland, and it started me thinking about the Fates might be doing now.

So not much in the way of tapestry reading these days - perhaps they're writers - write, edit and publish? Or more likely, consign to the eternal filing cabinet of doom.

By the time I got to *Fate in Your Hands*, they'd become bookshop owners. One of those shops you find down backstreets and alleyways - here today, gone tomorrow.

Where you can always find something to read because it contains every single story that ever has or will be written.

And because I'm the kind of person who wonders what characters are up to when you close the covers, imagining they down tools and enjoy a couple of quiet beers at the local pub. Or maybe tea and cake for the heroines, badmouthing the hero's personal hygiene...

And once the story is over? Do they go home and put their fluffy slippered feet up and rest until the next person opens the book?

They updated their names before I wrote *Fate in Your Hands*, and since then, they've been busy.

They've expanded their purview to parallel universes, got deeper in their engagement with humans, and started looking to spend more time apart.

First, Claudia questions whether she wants to give it all up.

Then Deirdre begs them to change the cir-cum-stances of her fate.

And just for fun, I've included *Fate in Your Hands*, the story that started it all; in which Erik grapples with returning to Norway to complete his military service.

Then Laura potentially meets the god of her dreams.

Marguerite escapes a serial killer and is reunited with her first love.

Finally, Agatha challenges Susan to change her unfortunate fate.

So, grab yourself appropriate beverage, sit back and put your fluffy slippered feet up, and enjoy the collection.

Alexandria Blaelock
Melbourne, Australia
September 2021

ALEXANDRIA BLAELOCK

FATE
OF THE
FATES

FATE OF THE FATES

Claudia put The Book of Fate aside, sighed, and pulled her red fox fur coat more closely around her. Then shook her long strawberry blonde hair around her for another layer of warmth.

Sure, it was nice enough, high up in the mountains, the air crisp and clear, and you could see for miles and miles around you.

As long as you didn't mind that the view was mainly snow, that the air was cold and crisp against your cheeks, and that the chill seeped into your bones no matter how many layers of clothes, or hair, you piled on.

Even the sound of birds flying overhead, and animals scurrying along the ground fell like stones; with a thud, disappearing into the snow's silence.

The two-room chalet she and her sisters lived in was mostly sealed against the wind, just the odd squeal as the wind gusted at speeds almost impossible to comprehend.

One of the rooms was full of Books; the sacred records of people's lives - past, present and future, this universe and all the others.

They lived in the other room.

Their beds were tucked under the eaves, closed in by doors that made the room look neater, kept the beds warmer, and provided an added layer of insulation.

Inside each cupboard, storage shelves were built into the walls at the end of the bed, and drawers for storing clothes underneath them.

The wooden walls and ceiling were dark with centuries of soot, waterproofing and use. The tiny windows set high in the walls.

In the centre of the room, was a fire.

Not like in the old days when the smoke from the open fire hung in the ceiling, but in a proper steel stove with a proper chimney that drew the smoke up and away.

Upon which a pot of venison and vegetable stew gently simmered filling the air with a delicious savoury fragrance.

Which almost completely hid the smell of dried apples, sultanas and cloves gently reconsti-tuting in another pot of water.

It was almost exactly perfect for a romantic get-away.

Aside from the never-ending presence of her sisters, and the complete absence of, well, a man.

Claudia allowed herself to dream a little about that nice blonde boy. Wherever it was he'd turned up. Somewhen in the middle of a dead-end red desert.

And then she looked at her sisters... No matter what, they couldn't compare.

Claudia was the youngest, Laura the middle, and Agatha the eldest. Though given they'd all been alive longer than time, that wasn't saying much.

Laura, her long black hair neatly pinned up and out of the way, currently dressed in black wolf skin, was polishing the measuring stick she used as a walking stick.

She'd been involved in some kind of accident before Claudia was born, and about which she re-fused to speak.

Agatha's short white bob brushed the polar bear coat she was wearing, making her look like a bear herself.

A fair warning to anyone else, as Agatha ate her prey alive as well.

Not literally of course, but she had a streak of ruthlessness about her, and it was best not to get on her bad side.

Though that wasn't entirely her fault, just something to be expected of someone whose job was to determine the time and circumstances of death.

As usual, she was sharpening her shears with a whetstone, the rhythmic snick, snick, snick of it loud in the quiet room.

Claudia stood up and took a step towards the stove to stir the pot of stew.

Tempted to eat just for something to do.

"Aren't you tired of sitting around here waiting for something to happen?"

"Not at all," said Agatha, "I'm happy just to be. Quietly, without any fuss."

Claudia rolled her eyes, but Agatha smiled insultingly sweetly.

"We're cosy enough here, and it really feels like we've been rushing around forever," said Laura.

"For heaven's sake! We could be doing noth-ing just as easily somewhere warm."

Her sisters started laughing.

"What?" said Claudia, but they just laughed harder.

"What?" she said, starting to get annoyed.

"Ah dear," said Agatha wiping her eyes, "we were just talking about when you'd be ready to leave."

"I won," said Laura, "hand it over," and Agatha fished a coin from her pocket and put it in Laura's outstretched hand.

"You're so predictable," she told Claudia.

"Where do you want to go this time?" Agatha asked.

"I don't know," Claudia's shrug was almost invisible under the fur, "somewhere warm. Maybe a beach?"

"Ah," said Laura, "we haven't been to a beach in a while."

Agatha grunted, though whether that was in agreement or not was another matter. "Perhaps somewhere uninhabited?"

"I'm not sure there's anywhere left that doesn't have someone living there," said Laura.

"There must be somewhere," said Agatha, "I'm not going unless there's no one there."

"I'll look into it," Claudia said, fluffing up her bedding, climbing into the cupboard and shutting the doors.

For a while, she heard them continuing the conversation as they prepared the chalet for travel, bickering amiably.

"Wouldn't you like to split up and take a vacation on your own one day?" asked Laura, banking the fire and tucking the pots underneath the stove.

"Hmmm, maybe. We'd need to go somewhere populated for that, and I'm not sure I could deal with so many people anymore." Agatha made the beds and tidied the sleeping cupboards.

"Could be fun," Laura swept the floor, sweeping the dirt and dust out into the snow.

"Maybe next time," Agatha opened the door to the book room, but as they hadn't used it for a while, it appeared in order.

And then they were done, they retired to their own beds to wait.

《《 • 》》

What Claudia hadn't told her sisters, was that the nexus was an ever-increasing network of universes.

Not just one.

And in all those universes, there was only one Claudia, but there were many many universes with and without versions of her sisters.

Perhaps because she was the only one in all the universes who wove the threads of fate into the full, glorious tapestry of life.

Or as some would have it, wrote the complete story of the universes.

That was what the book room was all about - hiding the life records where no one would think of stealing them.

Wherever they stopped they sold books for the money they needed to buy the other things they needed to survive.

Which wasn't much because the living room always reset to containing the things they needed to survive.

And they didn't sell THE books, but sometimes other books that Claudia brought from other times and places depending on what people needed at the time.

All those universes were getting a bit out of control, and she could really do with some help on that.

As each year passed, the universes expanded, and it got more and more difficult to find places they hadn't already visited. Though on occasion, if one universe deviated too much from its original root, she took the risk.

Not that it was chaotic as such in the nexus, but she enjoyed the time away from her sisters. There's nothing worse than being the youngest, forever, with older two sisters who are always picking on you, thinking you need to be monitored or instructed one way or another.

Even more galling when she had the power to erase them. Who cared about measuring or cutting when she could pull their threads out by the roots? Not that she wasn't tempted sometimes.

And they thought they were so smart...

Then again, she'd never told them she could travel the threads.

They knew she had something to do with it, but assumed the gods used her to send them where they needed to be, rather than her picking some more or less random place that looked nice.

The last few years she'd been searching for a copy of herself. Perhaps one she could swap with.

Or failing that, a nice man to live his life with while her sisters waited for her to come back.

They thought it just took the space of a nap, say an hour or two, but she'd been experimenting and had stayed away for six months without them noticing the difference.

It had been exhilarating. And liberating. And she wondered how long she could get away with this time.

She picked a thread at random and dove into it.

《《 • 》》

As always, her sensed returned slowly.

She heard booming, and for a moment was alone with the sound, trying to identify it.

The sound of surf crashing to the shore.

And then she heard seagulls squabbling.

She noticed she was warm. Too warm in the fur, but not quite awake enough to throw it off.

A sliver of blue sky through a gap in the wall.

The hint of some kind of herbal foliage blown in on the breeze through the gap.

And a little while later, the sound of her sisters talking, which was disappointing as she'd hoped to avoid them this time.

"Nice place," Laura said before taking a loud sip something, "house isn't bad either."

Agatha grunted in agreement. "How's Claudia?"

"Seems fine. No real way of telling."

"I'm worried by how much harder it seems to get each time."

Laura sipped again, "me too. I'm not sure what we can do to help her though."

"Is it something to do with The Book of Fate, or is it something she somehow figured out how to do on her own."

Laura shrugged, "no telling. But I can't help feeling like she needs some time on her own. A vacation of a sort."

Agatha grinned, "not like when we were young eh?"

"Speak for yourself, I'm not *that* old thank you very much."

"I suppose we could ask that old goat, whatever name he's going by now."

Claudia didn't care to hear anymore, and certainly didn't want them trying to fix her on what she'd hoped *would* be her vacation.

She struggled to get up, and out of the cupboard, and instantly her sisters were there to help her.

Out of the cupboard, into some fresh, clean, lightweight clothes and into her chair with a mug of tea and a bowl of venison stew.

Thankfully they didn't say anything, knowing she'd be out of sorts for a day or so after she'd moved them.

Never much for tact, Agatha said, "we're going out to see where we are."

And Laura, ever conciliatory, "you rest and we'll be back before you know it."

Claudia knew they'd be gossiping about her and plotting to visit "the old goat" whoever that was. She certainly didn't want any help from whoever he was.

But she'd have to stay for at least a week to get her strength back.

She took a sip of tea and looked around.

The structure of the room remained the same, but the walls were a bleached light wood and clean. The door and the large windows had been propped open to show a view of white sand, blue sky and turquoise ocean.

Tall trees grew down to the pristine white shore.

Setting aside the tea, she ate the stew.

There were worst places to recuperate, and it might not be so bad here for a while.

A bit of quiet for Agatha, and a slow pace for Laura.

Though she longed for the distractions of city life.

She finished her stew and took the remains of her tea outside to see where they were.

Her sisters were nowhere to be seen, but they'd banked a small fire in a shallow pit in the sand, the kettle left nearby.

Claudia was about to top up her tea when she saw a small boy walking along the shore towards her.

Tea forgotten, she watched him walk closer, wondering why he was there, and perhaps what fate he was hoping to dodge.

He approached more quickly than his short legs would suggest, but as he came closer, she realised he was not a boy, but a man.

With sun-bleached hair, and sun-darkened skin.

And muscles of the kind that come from hard work.

Wearing little more than a loincloth.

Walking with the grace and elegance of a panther, perhaps just as dangerous.

He stopped walking a couple of steps away, his arms by his sides and his hands relaxed, looking at her.

Closely.

Curiously.

Confidently.

At the same time as she was looking at him.

Avid. Assessing. Anxious.

She had the sense he could see through her, so she knew he wasn't from this world.

That perhaps the reason he knew, was that finally, she had found another her.

As he completed his examination, he turned and started walking away.

"Wait," she cried.

He stopped but didn't turn back, didn't move at all, just waited.

Nonplussed, she asked the only thing she could think of to stop him leaving, "what is your name?"

He turned his head toward her, and without looking at her said, "there is no need for you to know, as you will not see me again in this lifetime." And started walking again.

"Wait," she said, but he ignored her and kept walking.

He did not acknowledge her presence at all, and she was forced to drop the mug and run after him.

"Wait," she said catching hold of his arm, only to find her grip slid off him as he continued to walk.

"What do you mean in this lifetime?"

He paused for a fraction of a second, so small she barely noticed the check in his stride, and kept walking.

She ran ahead and stopped in his path, three-quarters afraid he'd walk through her body as if it didn't exist and out the other side. And that it would hurt.

But he stopped, considering her once more.

Then he sighed, and said, "you do not belong in this world."

"What makes you say that?"

"I can see your world wrapped around you like a cloak."

She thought about his word choice; wrapped around you like a cloak.

"More like wrapped around my throat like a noose.

"Have you met anyone else like this?"

"No," he said, looking at her with maybe a little more interest.

She put her hands on her hips, "how can you see my world anyway?"

He shrugged, "I don't know. I can just see that you are different to everyone else I have ever met."

"Is everyone else in this world like you?"

"I've never met anyone who is, but that doesn't mean they aren't out there."

She rubbed her eyes and looked at him again.

He didn't have a cloak wrapped around him, but there was something there. Some kind of au-ra.

A kind of buzzing, multicoloured electric aura. That might explain why her hand had slipped off his arm.

"There's something around you too. Some kind of energy that's alive. Something I've never seen before."

"Two of a different kind, but the same. What is this cloak that I see?"

"I am a weaver. My job... Or I suppose my calling is to weave the tapestry of life. My sisters measure and cut the threads."

"Ah, I see. I understand why the cloak is uneven. But why do you say it's like a noose around your neck?"

"Oh," she blushed. "It's all I've ever known, and the way my sisters talk, it's as if the universe would come to an abrupt end if I just let it go."

"I understand. You have no back up. The energy you see in me is the divine energy of this world that connects all creatures. All are one, and one is all, and no one is more important than any other one."

Claudia absently scratched her neck, "I find the idea of all as one oddly comforting. I wonder though, what would happen if I lost my connection to the threads."

"Do you want to find out?"

"Yes."

Without doubt or hesitation.

"Then let me see if I can sever the connection."

He put his hands around her throat, and she felt the burn of his divine energy.

He tightened his grip.

Claudia couldn't breathe and started to feel afraid.

She grappled to get a grip, to loosen his hands, but as with his arms, her hands could find no purchase and just slid off.

She wondered if she could die, and what that would be like. And as she lost consciousness, felt the tiniest bit of regret.

《《 • 》》

Claudia woke when the tide washed over her legs, with no idea how long the man had been gone, or what he'd done to her, or where she was.

The sun was descending towards a horizon of turquoise water. Tall trees grew down to the pristine white shore, and a light breeze blew down the coast bring the scent of some kind of flowers.

None of which offered any clues about what she was doing in that particular place at that particular time.

She knew there was something important she had to do. When she tried to remember what it was, she couldn't remember who she was Or why the thing she couldn't remember was so important.

She sat up and crawled a little further away from the tide line.

Cold, hungry, clueless.

Trying to work out what was next.

And where she lived.

Circling back to who she was.

Two old ladies were walking up the beach calling out for someone called Claudia, but she paid them no mind until one of them saw her, and started running towards her.

"Claudia, oh thank the gods we found you," the plump black-haired one said. She noticed that the hair on the left side of her head had fallen loose from the woman's bun.

"What the hell happened to you?" demanded the thin white-haired one.

Claudia struggled to close her mouth, then said, "do you know me?"

The women looked at each other, and then the white-haired woman shook her head and offered a hand to help her up. "We do know you, we're your sisters. Why don't you come with us so you can change your wet clothes and get something warm to eat?"

Claudia couldn't help looking at the other woman for confirmation. She nodded and offered her hand as well.

Claudia put up both her hands and allowed the two women to help her up.

The white-haired woman took off a white long-sleeved shirt and went to put it around Claudia's shoulders, and she shrugged it off, saying "don't!"

The old woman choked off a laugh, "at least you haven't forgotten everything."

Weirdly reassured, she followed the women until they disappeared into thin air in front of her.

She gaped, then slowly walked a few steps forward holding her arms out in front of her in case she ran into anything she couldn't see.

Then yelped in surprise as a voice behind her called "Claudia?"

She turned to see the black-haired woman apparently legless, leaning out of nothing.

"She can't see the house," she called to the white-haired woman who put her head out from nowhere to see.

"That's not possible," the white one said, walking further out from the nothing and becoming fully visible.

"Take my hand," she said, and tried to pull Claudia through the nothing to wherever it was the white-haired woman had come from, but the nothing resisted her; wouldn't let her through.

"Something's *really* wrong," she said to the black-haired woman. "We're going to have to get help."

"The night is drawing in; can't we wait until to-morrow?"

"I'm not sure that's wise. We can't take care of her while she's out here. Give me a hand and we'll see if the two of us can get her in here."

The two women, each taking one of her hands were not enough to pull her into the nothing.

"Claudia," said the white-haired woman, "tell me everything you can remember."

"Well, I woke on the beach, but before that...

"Well, I...

"Nope. Can't remember anything from before I woke up just then."

The two women looked at each other again, "Not me bringing you tea?" said the black-haired woman, "or helping you change?" said white.

The black-haired one disappeared and reappeared with some dry red clothes and a mug of something hot, "you know what to do."

They drew aside and watched her change her clothes. She heard something about powers, and stolen, and an old goat.

Though what a cloven-hoofed, ruminant animal had to do with anything she had no idea.

And then they speculated about whether the last trip was too much for her and she'd exhausted her powers.

Something about finding a place and fitting in.

When she'd changed, she looked at them helplessly as she drank her tea.

The white-haired one brought her a bowl of something deliciously savoury, and she let them argue about her some more.

She felt she ought to say something comforting, but there was nothing inside her head to say.

Given their hushed, but urgent tones, they were clearly concerned; trying not to alarm her. Though the whole situation was scaring her more the longer she listened.

What if she never remembered who she was?

What if she never made it back inside her invisible house?

The women seemed kind and concerned about her. Maybe even fond of her.

Now and again, they disagreed and looked at her as if she was the one who always broke the deadlock.

They definitely knew her, and she definitely played an important role in the way they looked at the universe *and* each other.

But she had no idea what.

She looked closely at each of them in turn, but felt no emotional response to either. They could have been anyone.

They *were* anyone. And she wondered whether she could sneak away from them before they noticed, because there was something about them that *really* bothered her.

She yawned, and just for a moment, closed her eyes.

«« • »»

When she woke on the beach the next morning, one or both of them had laid a blanket over her.

They had built a fire and were lying protective-ly either side of her around the fire.

She snuggled into her blanket, grateful they were near and she had not woken alone.

Her head ached as if someone was very slowly inserting a dagger into her skull. Then suddenly plunged it through, up to the hilt.

She would've screamed, or moved, but she was paralysed by the pain, and couldn't make a sound.

Shortly after that, she passed out.

«« • »»

When Claudia woke the second time, she thought perhaps it was a day later.

She bolted upright as she remembered what had happened. Scrambling to her feet and look-ing around her for the energy man, but he wasn't there.

She turned and looked at her sisters, and saw a tiny hint of multicoloured energy surrounding them, and wondered how they were connected to the divine energy of this world that connected all its creatures.

She looked more closely, and saw they were also connected to each other, and also to her with a red thread of energy, and relaxed. Strangely comforted.

Was he the personification of living energy?

Did that make her the personification of the fate of humanity?

Turning again, she saw the beach shack and understood it was her place. Where she belonged.

She put a pot of water on to boil, and was ready and waiting with tea when they woke.

Agatha examined her, "you're back then?"

Claudia smiled and resisted the temptation to hug her, knowing she'd hate that.

"Really?" asked Laura, and struggling out of her blanket, hugged Claudia, "thank the gods. What happened to you?"

"A stranger showed me my fate."

"Well that sounds positively creepy, should we move somewhere else?" asked Laura.

"Definitely," said Agatha.

"But we came here for you," said Claudia, "somewhere slow-paced and quiet!"

"After yesterday's events, I'd rather not stay here any longer than strictly necessary," Laura declared.

"Agreed," said Agatha, "if you feel up to it."

And oddly, she did, so she nodded.

"Somewhere busy this time," said Agatha.

"Maybe a city where we can go to a show or two," Laura agreed.

Claudia smothered a smile.

They doused the fire and took the blankets and other gear back into the beach shack.

She climbed into her sleeping cupboard as her sisters cleaned up and prepared the shack for travel.

Taking a deep breath, she relaxed into the nexus.

She looked into the tapestry, tracing the thread she'd just emerged from, trying to decide whether to pull it out.

But it unravelled itself and disappeared in a flash of energy.

Which should have annoyed her, but she felt happier that this decision at least had been taken out of her hands.

She picked another thread and followed it, hoping this one would take her back to her sis-ters.

THE END

ALEXANDRIA BLAELOCK

FATE OR FOE

Deirdre paced around the edges of the randomly coloured and patterned carpet that sat in the cen-tre of the wooden floor of her room as she con-templated the nature of fate.

Her fate in particular.

Her seemingly unavoidable fate.

For one thing, her name was Deirdre. The broken-hearted.

What kind of irresponsible parent would gift that name to a child - no matter how influential the namesake.

As a second thing, her parents had found an "advantageous" match for her, and she was being shipped off to another country to marry a stranger.

Leaving everything she knew behind.

So, to be completely honest, not all that advantageous to her.

The advantageous match in question had not bothered to introduce himself to her, either in person or by letter.

Clearly, he had no regard, and precious little concern for her, so how exactly was that advantageous to her?

And if that wasn't bad enough, her parents were trying to convince her he'd seen her at a party (when she wasn't permitted to go anywhere), and had fallen in love with her, and was too shy to reach out to her.

Did they think she was an idiot?

Real-life did not consist of fairy tale endings.

As if to mock her, a pair of brightly coloured birds swooped past her tower window, calling sweet nothings to each other. Seemingly intent on the Spring mating season.

This new match was certainly nowhere near as advantageous as Ethan, for example, who was very concerned with her health and welfare.

So much so she'd been charmed and snuck out of the manor to spend generous amounts of alone time with him in the forest.

So much time she'd gone way passed charmed, bypassing infatuated, straight to falling in love with, and wanting to run away from her responsibilities with him.

Though it had to be said, he was a lot less keen on her now she was betrothed to another.

You had to wonder whether he had actually liked her at all.

For a third, she was stuck in her bedroom.

Not exactly forbidden to leave, but with guards posted on the outside, presumably to protect what was now a *valuable* asset, certainly not allowed to roam as freely as she had before the betrothal.

It wasn't a particular hardship; it was a nice enough room as far as rooms go. She paused to list its positives as if she was trying to sell it:

A spacious ten by twelve paces.

Bright and well-lit, with several small embrasures.

Airy, yet cosy.

Easily defensible.

Pristine white walls and ceiling that bounced the light around.

Plenty of books to amuse herself with when she didn't want to do any needlecraft.

Which was always, causing no end of trouble with the state of her hand-stitched trousseau.

And her mother's nerves.

Deirdre's younger sister Cara (the beloved) would have traded places with her in an instant.

They'd done their best to persuade their parents, but to no avail.

For some ridiculous reason or another, the advantageous match required the eldest daughter, not the younger.

Or any other daughter should there be more than two.

Not to mention that tradition described the marriages from eldest to youngest, with Cara remaining at home forever to take care of her parents while their eldest brother ran amok being the local laird.

In so many ways, a tragic turn of events for *all* involved parties.

Though, in theory, not her problem.

Anymore.

Deirdre took another lap of the carpet.

Cara was propped on Deirdre's bed, examining her red hair for split ends, snipping them off with a tiny pair of scissors attached to her châtelaine.

Now and again, she gave in and peeled one back, trying to get it the length of the strand.

"I've heard there's a place you can go to beg the Fates to change it," she said idly.

Deirdre took five paces, and flung herself on the bed at the opposite end to her sister.

Who was hogging the pillows and presumably leaving splinters of hair there as well.

"And?" she said.

Cara paused, lock of hair in one hand and scis-sors in the other, looking at her sister. She shrugged, "that's all I know."

Deirdre slapped Cara's closest leg to her, "you would have to be the most useless person I know."

"It's a shame mother doesn't feel that way."

Cara dropped the trimmed hair and sectioned out another lock. "I don't know what you're complaining about anyway. I'd do about anything to get out of here."

"I know," Deirdre groaned, "we *all* know."

Too restless to settle, she picked herself up and started pacing again, "who told you about this place where the Fates receive petitioners?"

"I overheard the laundry maids gossiping. Apparently, they have a shop. Somewhere in town. I think they said it was a tapestry shop."

"And what are their fees?"

Cara shrugged again, "I don't know. Proportional I guess. Depending on what fate you're trying to avoid, and what you're willing to accept instead."

Deirdre bent down, trying to look in Cara's eyes, "you do realise this is almost the exact answer to our problems?"

"'Spose."

Deirdre growled impatiently, "I despair of you, really I do. We could have been rid of this, and you haven't even prepared an escape route."

"I don't need to," she screwed her face into a mocking, smiling mask, "you're so desperate you'll do it for me."

And that was true.

Cara did nothing.

Ever.

Beloved by name, and utterly charming when she wanted something.

No one was immune.

Beloved she might be, but utterly ruthless in getting anything that took her fancy.

Leaving a trail of carnage in her wake; the corpse of a puppy she'd coveted, the burn-scarred face of a love rival, and the boy who'd been besotted with the burned face had mysteriously fallen from the tower.

Deirdre asked all the laundry maids until she found out where the Fate's shop was.

Though in the end, she had to say Cara want-ed to know because *everyone* knew how she felt about her life.

And everyone thought Deirdre couldn't be anything less than over the moon happy that some guy (who she was sure had never seen her) should be so in love with her that nothing would satisfy him but that she marry him with haste.

And yeah, sure, she was living the fairy tale.

But.

She wanted a *real* life.

On her own terms.

According to the maids, the shop was in another city, about half a day's ride away.

She didn't expect she'd be coming home, but for a plausible excuse, she'd have to stay away overnight.

And that excuse would have to be reputable.

She could go shopping, but there wasn't any kind of industry in the city that might attract a Lady.

Or visit a shrine to pray and purify herself for the marriage. Assuming there was one there.

And that was another thing that bothered her about the marriage.

Despite the tradition of marrying in the bride's home town, he'd demanded she travel to his. Without her family.

Or a bridal procession.

In fact, he'd sent a squad of armed guards to fetch her.

Though it didn't altogether matter whether there was a shine or not.

If she said there was one, her mother would believe her.

Because Deirdre had always taken her responsibilities seriously.

Always done what she was told.

And always confessed when she had done something to disappoint them.

Nonetheless, she quizzed the laundry maids further and discovered that there was a shrine.

Even better, for the goddess Áine - goddess of love, wealth and Summer.

Handy.

Deirdre knew she'd have to sacrifice her honesty at some point, but didn't want to have to lie any more than she had to.

She couldn't sit comfortably with it.

At least not yet.

So that was the first plan. To boldly seek permission to travel to the next city to receive a blessing. She shuddered just thinking about it,

Then squared her shoulders, and stood tall, spine straight; failing that, sneak out.

But much easier if she could go openly.

The next issue was how she might be able to slip away from her guards.

Presumably, she'd need a woman's excuse. Some kind of ritual where men weren't welcome.

She continued her enquiries.

And it happened there *was* a Druidic community nearby that could offer a pretext for some alone time. Though how to get from there to the tapestry shop was another question.

Or even where the tapestry shop was.

With the date of departure rapidly closing in, she had no real choice but to just get on with it.

Telling her parents turned out to be no trouble.

Going away for a night of ritual purification was fine with them, as long as she took her sister along with her.

And came back ready, and willing to stop with the sad face and miserable attitude, and travel to her new husband without further delay or complaint.

Slipping the guards was nowhere near as easy.

The guards sent with her were not those she'd grown up with, prepared to let her get away with a modicum of misbehaviour, but those her husband-to-be had sent.

Any shred of humanity concealed by their warlike armour and closed helmets.

Always assuming they were actually human.

After being denied entry to the community, they set up camp insultingly close to the boundaries. So close, they were right up against the hedging that surrounded it.

And her sister, as her only attendant, was no help whatsoever.

"I can't wait to see what you do next."

It was so tempting to leave her behind.

In the end, she sacrificed her honesty and stole some servant's clothes from the washing line.

And then her hair, hacking it off after a slight hesitation, so she looked like a boy.

A boy with a clean, soft face wouldn't do at all, so she rubbed ash on her cheeks and chin to disguise that.

Deirdre knew it would be worth it.

And if there were no fates, and she couldn't make a deal, then hopefully she'd get far enough away before her betrothed's guards got suspicious about the delay.

A maximum of 24 hours on foot.

How long did it take a horse to gallop that far?

Or could she hide in plain sight - did the guards know what she looked like, or did they just see the outward trappings?

Better to pray to each and every deity that the Fates existed, *and* were willing to make a deal.

Sacrificing her dignity she dressed in the boy's clothes, then sacrificed her poise, fruitlessly begging her sister to dress in the servant's clothes.

Then begging her to leave via the mendicant's gap in the hedge.

But Cara's dignity would only be satisfied by walking out the front door.

So Deirdre sacrificed even her status, following Cara as if she was her sister's servant.

She kept her eyes on the ground as the guards attempted to stop Cara, who pointed out they had nothing to do with her and her shopping plans.

Reminding them their duty lay with Deirdre, who was safely inside observing the marriage blessing rituals.

They grumbled suspiciously, but in the end, they had no real choice but to let her, and the "boy" leave.

Deirdre followed her meekly, allowing her to walk several paces ahead.

Mostly for the show of it, and only a little so she was forced to control her temper.

Even when Cara slowed to allow her to catch up, Deirdre slowed as well to remain a few paces behind her.

Cara found the tapestry shop, and Deirdre had the idea she'd known where it was all along.

Three women were sitting on a long bench outside the store.

The youngest, whose strawberry blond hair hung loosely around her shoulders declaring her to be a maiden, wore a red dress.

She was holding a piece of fine embroidery in her lap, the needle pushed through a corner so it didn't get lost.

The dark-haired woman's face was sun worn. She wore a wimple and a black dress, suggesting a widow. She was flicking a measuring stick around the fingers of one hand.

The final woman was wearing her white hair in a crown of plaits around her head, and a spotless white gown. She radiated a sense of eternity but looked about the same age as the red-haired woman. She was sharpening a pair of shears.

"I demand to see the Fates," said Cara.

The women didn't acknowledge her. The red-headed woman leaned to her right, and the black and white-haired women to the left, looking around Cara at Deirdre.

Deirdre knew they were judging her, and as she was sincere in her desire to seek their favour, she bowed deeply.

They looked at each other for a moment, then the white-haired woman stood up and walked into the store.

Cara attempted to follow her, but Deirdre held her back until the others had followed the white-haired woman in.

Only then did she drop her arm, allowing Cara to go in.

As Deirdre entered the store, she felt a kind of flicker. As though somehow, the interior they entered was not attached to the facade.

Or perhaps somewhere else entirely.

The room inside was lighter than she ex-pected, and she saw no end to it.

A tapestry hung along the wall on her left, a seething mix of threads that wouldn't let her eyes settle on any one point.

As she looked along the tapestry, which seemed to stretch further that the endless room, she could almost make sense of it.

She heard something like a bird flutter, and looked up to see hundreds, if not thousands of small glowing tapestries hanging from the ceiling.

It reminded her a little of the Great Hall at home, the banners of the knights, both dead and alive, suspended from the beams.

While they did not glow, the suspended tapestries were obviously the source of the light. Deirdre had no idea how, or why, they were glowing.

Cara was right behind the women as they walked further into the space, but Deirdre stopped every few paces to look at the racks of different coloured threads dripping into the enormous vats of dye.

She tripped over an uneven flagstone and realised they'd started talking and she hadn't noticed.

She hurried to catch up.

The redheaded woman turned to Cara and asked, "what is it you want?"

"I want to be Deirdre," she said, almost before the woman had finished speaking.

"Cara!" Deirdre roared, though she couldn't have said whether she was more shocked by her impudence, or that she was too dense to come up with something of her own; preferring to take Dierdre's life.

As if it was as easy as changing her gown.

"What?" Cara put her hands on her hips, the classic tell she was preparing for a fight. "If you get your way, you won't be here.

"And if you get your way, then I'll get what I want."

It was true that Cara had always wanted whatever Deirdre had, but to hear her say out loud, that she wanted your life, was another thing en-tirely.

Still, Cara was right.

And Deirdre had no right to be so mean-spirited about it. She should allow herself to be glad; Cara might be happier that way.

She straightened her shoulders and looked at the woman. "Fine, I'm prepared to walk away from it all."

Cara smiled like a cat with cream; not that Deirdre had ever seen a cat smile, cream or no cream.

As she watched, Cara just faded away, as if she had never been born.

And technically she hadn't.

"What will happen to Cara now?"

"You have no need to know," the white-haired one said.

The black-haired one tutted, "No need for that Agatha." Taking Deirdre's arm, she drew her across to a vat of blue dye and waved her hand over the surface.

Deirdre leaned over the surface to see.

《《 • 》》

Deirdre paced around the edges of the random colour patterned carpet that sat in the centre of the wooden floor of her room as she contemplat-ed the nature of fate.

Broken-hearted by name.

Broken-hearted by nature.

Being shipped off to marry a stranger who hadn't even sent a letter for her with the proposal

Stuck in her bedroom without so much as a younger sister to help pass the time...

《《 • 》》

"Well that's not going to end well," said Aga-tha.

Deirdre grabbed her arm, "what do you mean?"

"It's not your fate anymore, why do you care?"

"I don't want Cara to get hurt.

Agatha smiled a straight lipped smile, "you heard her, she said she wanted to be you."

"But—"

"Not the eldest daughter, or your replacement, but you. *Specifically*, you."

And then she turned to the black-haired woman, "though I fear I've messed things up a little for you."

"Well, you *were* a little cruel. Anyway, it's nothing much. I can make it work."

"So what happens when someone wants to be them, and the original wants to be themselves?" Deirdre asked.

"Same thing as will happen to you," the redhead said, walking across to the vat, "we find them new, unoccupied circumstances and erase their memories as we go."

"Then I won't remember being me?"

"No one does dear," said the black-haired woman, "we don't leave any lingering regrets.

"Now, what do we do about you? What kind of life are you looking for?" said the white-haired woman.

"You're asking me?"

"Of course dear," said the black-haired woman, "what's the point otherwise."

"Oh," Deirdre said blushing, "I thought you'd just look me over and assign something."

The women looked at each other.

The white-haired woman snorted, and the redhead turned away, her shoulders shaking. The black-haired woman chuckled, turning it to a laugh and couldn't stop.

The redhead couldn't contain it and started laughing, and set the white-haired one off too.

She clutched Deirdre's shoulder, and as if it was a virus, she was laughing too.

With no idea why.

Eventually, the women got a hold of themselves.

"Ah that was good," said the white-haired one sighing.

The black-haired one rubbed her sides, "I haven't laughed like that in centuries."

The redhead was still trying to catch her breath.

"What did I say?"

"Most people," said the white-haired one gasping, "have a very definite idea before they get here."

"Ah. I thought that would be presumptuous of me."

And that started them off again.

While they laughed, Deirdre started thinking about what kind of life she wanted, and by the time they stopped had prepared a list.

"Okay then. I want to be someone ordinary," the women looked away from each other.

"And I want to love and be loved. Marry someone who sees me as an equal partner. To make a difference."

"That's quite a wish list, but I think we can manage it," the redhead said.

The women linked hands, and the air shimmered.

As the room faded around Deirdre, she thought she might have heard one say "you know she's going to die anyway, right?"

And another reply, "yes, but this time it'll mean something."

The scene rushing toward her was terrifying.

«« • »»

A city street, full of mirrored towers that filled the sky. It was loud, *really* loud, and she felt the brightness of the lights must surely burn through her eyeballs and singe her brain.

A line of men in black uniforms were arrayed before her. They carried almost imperceptible shields on one arm and held nasty looking black cudgels in the other.

She wasn't sure who they were, but they had the look of seasoned warriors. Something about the way they carried themselves; firm, yet light on their feet.

The air was thick with smoke, and some weird and metallic smell within it was making her gag.

She was hot, packed in a large crowd of sweat-soaked people, jostling around her.

"Gilda," someone cried, "Gilda snap out of it. The cops are coming."

Gilda shook herself and squared her shoulders. "I'm here to demonstrate my democratic right to peacefully protest. The only way those thugs are going to get me out, is in a body bag."

THE END

AUTHOR OF THE HISTORIES OF HAYWARD HALL
ALEXANDRIA
BLAELOCK

FATE
IN YOUR
HANDS
A SHORT STORY

FATE IN YOUR HANDS

Erik looked out at a seemingly endless vista of red desert, broken here and there by tussocks of spinifex.

Way off in the distance, through the shimmering heat haze, stood the odd stumpy tree.

It was hotter than it had any right to be; beating down from the sun high overhead and radiating up from the ground.

The hot air tasted like dry sand and seemed to pull all the moisture from his lungs.

Sighing, he turned to look the dilapidated weatherboard building under a sign reading "Last bookshop 1000 km."

He could tell it had been a handsome and proud home in its young glory days, but now it leant drunkenly on rotten stumps, held together by termite nests.

That it stood at all was a miracle, but that the wide veranda supported the weight of a long slatted wooden seat and the three women looking curiously at him was a wonder.

The youngest, in scarlet shorts and tank top, sat cross-legged on the left. She was in her early twenties, and her long strawberry blond hair was caught up in a messy bun on the top of her head.

She held a book in her lap, with a finger tucked in the spine to mark her place.

The woman in the middle was maybe 40. She looked tired, and her long dark hair hung loosely around her shoulders. Her black semi-fitted dress must have been stifling in the heat.

She was leaning forward, resting her chin on her folded hands on a walking stick.

On the right was a stunning woman with short white hair that seemed to dance in the rising heat. She might have been 22, 45, or maybe even 100. She sat upright yet relaxed; one leg crossed over the other. Amazingly, her loose white pants and button-down shirt were untaint-ed by the red dust that piled up around the base of the walls.

She was idly trimming her fingernails with a small pair of scissors.

They looked at each other for a long moment before Erik shook himself and walked towards the building.

The woman in red unfolded herself from the seat and stood to meet him. That her skin could be so white in the outback was an incredible feat.

"Diana from the Palace Hotel sent me," he said. His English was good, but his Scandinavian accent fell heavily into the still air.

The young woman smiled and turned to open the door for him.

"All the books are mixed together - new and second hand in all the languages we have."

She pointed to the right, "fiction is over there," and then to the left, "non-fiction there.

"All our available stock is out, so please don't ask if we have anything else.

"Take your time, we'll be here out the front if you find something you like."

Then she turned away, leaving him in the open doorway.

He leaned forward slightly, expecting a small room with an even smaller stack of books, but in-stead there was an enormous room of modern shelving crammed with books.

And even more books stacked on the floor between the shelves.

Books so far as the eye could see, it was almost as if every book ever printed had been stuffed into the room.

He leaned back out to look across the width of the building before leaning back in to compare. The room was definitely bigger inside than the building.

Leaning back out, he looked at the women, who were looking at him quizzically.

The one in white made an impatient gesture towards the interior.

He smiled tentatively and nodded at them before taking a deep breath and stepping across the threshold.

Immediately he turned around, and was reassured by the continuing existence of the open door, and the view of the desert.

A flock of black cockatoos flew past screeching.

While it all seemed normal, he wanted to put his hand out the door, just to make sure it was really was a doorway and that it really was there.

Taking another deep breath, this time of book scented air, he turned towards the fiction.

His working holiday visa had almost expired, and it was time to head home to fulfil his mandatory Military Service quotient.

He'd been monitoring the political situation, and tensions had been escalating while he was away. He'd waited so long that he was just about out of time to enlist.

Perhaps if he'd joined up straight out of school, he'd have been safe, but it seemed almost certain he'd see active service on his return.

He looked at the long rows of shelves.

What he needed was something to take his mind off the fear. Something like an epic hero saga. Or a man who snatched success from the jaws of defeat.

A man who overcame his fate.

As he browsed the stacks, he could hear the faint, yet oddly comforting sound of the women's voices from the verandah.

It was kind of like being in his room as a child, hearing his mother and aunts in the kitchen, gossiping about the village as they preserved fresh produce for the winter.

He smiled slightly remembering a time he'd sat on the stairs eavesdropping. And without really thinking, he found himself listening to the women outside.

"What do you think?"

"I think he needs our help Claudia, but he has to ask for it."

"Well that's a bit harsh don't you think Agatha?"

"No such thing as a free lunch Laura."

"But Agatha—"

"Enough, we're not fairies here to grant wishes."

"Agatha, no one is saying anything about wishes."

"For heaven's sake Claudia, we can't just go around meddling in the lives of mortals. We're not gods."

"I didn't mean it like that."

"Well, what did you mean then?'

"Well, um, just that there's asking and there's asking."

"Honestly, you're slow as a wet week Claudia."

"Please Agatha. What about *earning* a favourable indulgence?"

"That's really not helping Laura."

"No really, why not?"

"Or couldn't he buy a favour with a gift?"

"Agatha, for once in your life, will you just think about it?"

"Shh. He's listening."

Silence immediately fell, as if someone had hit a cosmic mute button.

Not that he should have been eavesdropping, but it seemed everywhere he went in this country, people stopped talking when he walked into the room.

Now he was starting to think it might be him and not something that all people who live in remote towns do when strangers walk in.

What help did they expect him to ask for?

Choosing a book?

At which point, it seemed a suitably thick book jiggled on the shelf to attract his attention.

It was a dusty old hardback, the knife cut edges of its slightly textured pages were yellowed, and dog earned.

He opened the cover, and the aroma of cigar smoke, cologne and adventure rose from its pages. The vivid frontispiece of a Viking longship riding stormy seas was strangely compelling.

He flicked through the pages at random and found himself pulled into a mythic retelling of the saga of Erik the Red. He gently closed the cover and weighed the book in his hand.

Its size and weight fit comfortably into his palm, in fact, the book seemed to nestle into his hand like a lost puppy.

It seemed the perfect book had found him.

Turning to retrace his steps, he realised he'd lost sight of the door and wasn't entirely sure where it was.

Not that it isn't always possible to get lost in a good bookshop.

But given this one seemed larger than the building that housed it, it felt a more disastrous situation than one might usually suppose.

Erik giggled nervously, should he have set a string line for guidance when he struck out from the main corridor?

Clutching *Erik the Red* like a talisman and trying to swallow his panic, he reasoned that if he could hear the women talking, they couldn't be that far away.

If fiction was on the right, all he had to do was follow the path to the left, no matter how far it went, and it would lead him back to the door.

Straightening his pack on his shoulders, he clutched the book to his chest and started walking.

After a time, Erik wondered if it really was as simple as keeping to the left.

He didn't feel any closer to the door than before. The shelves were starting to look the same; lurid splashes of red and blue-toned covers with seemingly hallucinogenic gilt embossed collections of letters and symbols on the spines.

He saw a flash of red heading to the right and thinking it was the girl, chased after her.

Heart pounding, teetering on the cusp of turning the corner, he felt doubt creeping in.

Should he trust himself, or follow the girl he'd just met?

Was she trying to help him?

Was it even her, or just his imagination?

He closed his eyes, took a deep breath and held it until he could hear his blood pumping and then slowly let it out.

Choosing to believe in himself, he continued his path to the left.

He started to feel as though the shelves were closing in on him, and he couldn't catch his breath.

The back of his neck started prickling as though someone was creeping up on him.

He spun around, heart pounding wildly in his chest, but there was no one there.

The book was a solid and reassuring presence in his arms.

If Erik the Red could trust himself and take a boat into the unknown, so could he.

Mind you, Erik hadn't gone alone, he'd taken a crew to help. Each crew member had their own function, and together they'd travelled beyond the known universe and for the most part, come safely back.

Perhaps that had been what the women had been talking about. If you need help, you have to ask for it.

"Um, excuse me," he called.

The woman in black immediately stepped out from the shelves in front of him, "yes?"

Erik squeaked and stepped back.

The woman smiled faintly.

He coughed, trying to give the impression he was just clearing his throat.

"I'm sorry, you startled me. I've found a book, but I need help getting to the checkout."

"This way please," she said, disappearing around the shelving unit on his left.

He followed and found her leaning on her stick, waiting for him in a wide-open space be-tween the shelves.

Convinced the gap he'd passed through wouldn't be there if he turned around, he focused on the startlingly ordinary country town shop in front of him.

To one side, a fridge full of cold drinks and chocolate bars hummed gently.

It was nestled between a display unit of assorted dried packaged snacks and a bent up revolving wire rack of postcards, souvenir magnets, keyrings and spoons.

On the other, an old manual cash register sat on one end of a wooden counter next to a stack of tissue paper held down by a rock.

A wall-mounted rotary fan ruffled the paper as it blew from side to side across the room.

It was all reassuringly ordinary.

And that was sort of unsettling.

Given the bigger on the inside room and the never-ending book stacks, paying and leaving wasn't going to be as easy as it looked.

He walked to the counter with the woman and passed her the book.

She weighed it in her hand; "nice choice. Did you know this is the only book he wrote?"

Erik shook his head.

"The author died shortly after it was published."

"Really? How did he die?"

"Mustard Gas poisoning, in the trenches during the First World War. It's an ugly way to die."

Erik shuddered. "I wish I didn't know that. I'm on my way home to complete my Military Service." And having chosen, I can move forward.

"Not to worry, they don't use gas these days."

He attempted a smile, "no, I suppose not. But there are still plenty of ugly ways to die in a war zone."

She took the rock off the paper and started wrapping the book. "Yes that's true. Though people die without going to war too you know."

"I guess so. I just wish the political situation at home was more stable."

She smiled sadly, "yet even knowing the risk, you're on your way home to fulfil your duty."

He smiled back, "if it's my fate to die during my service, then there's not much use fighting it is there?"

"Maybe not, but you'd be surprised just how many people do fight against their fates.

"I think it's courageous to do what you know you must, even when you're afraid of the outcome."

Erik snorted, "is it courage, or is it social pressure?"

She laughed, "I'll concede that social pressure does make a difference, but you still have to choose. Safeguarding the fates of others can never be the worst possible decision."

There's no more reason to stand still, worrying about what's the right thing to do."

"Just so."

"Imagine that! A trip to the outback to talk Vikings and debate Kierkegaard."

She laughed again and having finished wrapping the book, sealed it with a round sticker.

"It's a bookshop in the middle of the desert, where else are you going to talk about the things that scare you?"

She put the book in a thick paper bag, pulled out the straw handles and offered it to him.

"How much do I owe you?"

"Nothing. Just take it, and get home safely."

"I can't do that, how are you supposed to make a living if you just give the stock away? You must let me pay for it."

She pursed her lips for a moment as she thought. "Well, if you're determined, perhaps you could help out with a little something that's been troubling us?"

He nodded eagerly.

"There's a big spider in the outhouse, and we'd be so grateful if you could get it out."

Erik swallowed nervously, "don't Australian spiders kill?"

She laughed again, "even if we had those kinds of spiders here, Dr Kennedy has antivenom at the surgery, and that's only an hour's drive away."

He rocked his head from side to side and reset his shoulders.

"All right, I can do this. You'd better show me where it is before I change my mind."

"I'll show you," the voice from behind him made him jump. Turning, he came face to face with the woman in white.

Her face was still and unreadable as she led him out a door he hadn't noticed before. She didn't speak as she led him down a well-worn path from the back of the building.

Silently, she pointed at the outhouse.

Its wooden walls were bleached light grey by the sun, and what remained of its door hung stiffly at an angle from one hinge. A toilet, the old-fashioned kind of lidded box with a hole in it was clearly visible.

The whole thing was festooned in spider web as though wrapped for Christmas.

He tried not to imagine a gigantic spider crawling over its roof to eat him as a snack.

"So. Are we talking about a spider as big as a saucer, or a spider as big as a mill wheel?"

The old woman snorted, "I'm pretty sure it's not even as big as the palm of my hand, but it is fast."

"Does it have a favourite spot?"

"Well, here in Australia they tend to live in small spaces, like under rocks, or between the bark and tree trunks."

"That's interesting, why do they do that?"

"Can't you feel the heat out here? During the day it's too hot to hunt, so they just hang around waiting for food to show up."

"Oookaay." He removed his backpack and dropped it to the ground. It was time to battle the monster.

He dodged back and forward a few times like a boxer and tried not to shudder in front of the old woman.

"I can do this," he said, more for his benefit than hers.

She started backing towards the house, "I'll wait for you back here."

He approached the outhouse slowly and cautiously. Still not exactly sure what he was looking for, he walked around the structure, closely inspecting the exterior walls.

Finding nothing, he had no choice but to enter it.

But for a moment, he stood still, peering inside, summoning the courage to do so.

Was it foolhardy to continue?

Could he sneak off leaving the book behind?

He discreetly glanced over his shoulder to see the old woman leaning nonchalantly, hands in her pants pockets, against the shop's back wall.

No escape that way then.

Anyway, it was just a spider, even if it was a man-eating Australian spider, how hard could it be?

Erik stood in the doorway, he licked his lips, then closed his eyes for a few seconds to give them a chance to adjust to the gloom.

He was surprised, it didn't smell unpleasantly like human excrement, more like dirt and air. It was bearable.

Opening his eyes again he looked around the interior, and saw nothing that looked like a spider.

Remembering what the old woman said about spiders living under things, he casually lifted the lid with one foot and was shocked when a spider as big as his foot launched itself from beneath it.

Momentarily paralysed by fear, he squealed as it landed on his foot. Then started screaming as it held on while he tried to hop backwards out of the toilet and flick it off at the same time.

Just as he made it out, falling over backwards, the spider flew off his foot and turning a somersault scurried off into a spinifex plant.

Erik lay screaming for an instant longer as the old woman laughed.

She trotted up the path and helped him to his feet.

"You're fine, you're fine. You've saved us from the giant monster."

He whimpered for a moment but straightened up as the other women approached.

"You've done well Erik," the old woman said, resting her hand lightly on his shoulder.

The youngest picked up his backpack and helped him into it, then the middle-aged one handed him his book bag.

"We've tested you three times," the old woman continued, "and each time you've proved yourself a man capable of facing your fear, adapting and growing."

She smiled a warm and loving smile.

"You *will* survive all that your destiny throws at you. You'll not only survive but thrive, living a long and happy life this time around.

"We're so proud of you.

"Now go back to town, and have a beer on us."

He nodded and started walking down the road, back to the town.

He was exhausted, it had been a long day, and a couple of beers in a loud, noisy bar would be just the thing before catching the bus back to the Big City in the morning.

He shuddered for a moment thinking about the spider, before enjoying the warm glow of fac-ing and defeating his fear.

But something niggled at him, how did the old woman know what his name was?

He turned back, but as he half expected, the bookshop was gone.

Only the desert remained, crisscrossed by skit-tered lizard tracks.

He smiled, surviving and thriving was what it was all about then.

He'd survived this, he could survive anything.

THE END

ALEXANDRIA BLAELOCK

IT MUST BE FATE

A SHORT STORY

IT MUST BE FATE

Laura bustled down the city street, sleek black handbag over one shoulder, stilettos clacking on the pavement.

Her shoulder-length black hair was smoothed back into an unravelling ponytail which swung from side to side with each step she took.

She looked the peak of efficiency in her slightly too tight black suit; anyone who looked at her would have thought she was at the pinnacle of her Personal Assistant career.

Perhaps her boss was the CEO of a medium-sized company who'd taken her with him to the top.

But she was uncomfortably aware she was perspiring, her feet were killing her, and she just wanted the time to sit somewhere, slip her shoes off and enjoy a *very* large, *very* cold and preferably alcoholic drink.

She balanced a packet of tomato sauce flavoured chips on top of her mobile phone in her left hand, crushing handfuls into her mouth with her right as she walked.

Not for the first time, she thought losing weight might be a good thing, but she just didn't have the time.

Not like the old days when she'd enjoyed cooking from scratch and taking long treks through the countryside hunting game.

And her sisters were useless - no help whatsoever.

Maybe next time they should go to Tokyo or Seoul where you could get healthier meals and snacks in every corner store.

Much more convenient, and so easy to keep the weight off.

Glass skyscrapers towered above her on all sides, reflecting the summer light and heat towards each other, and anyone unfortunate to be walking or waiting beneath them.

The air, barely cooled by the wind tunnelling along the street brought grit, sheets of newspaper, and empty chip packets with it.

She dropped her own empty packet into a bin, and the wind lifted it out again, threw it at her and then further on down the street where it joined a maelstrom of others.

Still walking, she lifted a handkerchief from her bag, wiped her hands on it and carefully put it back in case the wind took it as well.

She paused at a traffic light to check her phone.

In many ways, it was so handy to receive people's wishes by text, or perhaps a phone call now and again, but it was *too* easy for them.

She'd had to turn off the ring *and* the vibration, because it was a constant torment of noise.

In the old days, they'd wait for people to come to them, and because the journey was arduous, they didn't unless they had meaningful concerns.

She'd had the time to eat and exercise, and keep the house immaculately clean.

But now...

There was nowhere to hide out of reach, people used their wishes recklessly, and she couldn't keep up with them.

Let alone keeping the house in order and taking care of herself.

Not for the first time, she contemplated how much happier she might have been in an ordinary finite life.

A life full of all the frivolous concerns people had these days.

She started flicking through the texts:

Yes, doing well at the job interview.

No, definitely pregnant.

Yes, passing exams.

No, he doesn't like you; he's just scamming you.

Yes, she does like you; obsessively so.

She heard the lights change to walk, took a step forward and still focused on her phone, tripped over the curb.

Arms wheeling, she tried to save herself, but it looked like the ground was coming closer towards her anyway.

At the last possible minute, someone who smelled fresh and citrusy grabbed her arm, pulling her up, twisting her around and setting her on her feet.

A man.

A gorgeous man.

In an immaculately tailored navy-blue pinstripe suit. With a white shirt and matching vest if you please. A slim silver and blue diagonal stripe tie completed the picture.

His short, dark hair was neat and completely unaffected by the wind. It didn't look weighed down with product, nor did it look as though he'd spent any time in the bathroom blow-drying it.

Clean-shaven, with intriguingly green eyes.

Laura realised she was staring open-mouthed at him. For a woman a thousand years old (rounding down), not a good look.

She shut her mouth with a snap and directed her gaze to the ground.

Where she couldn't help but notice his narrow-toed shoes were highly shined.

And felt fat and frumpy by contrast. And of course, at that moment, noticed some kind of stain on the skirt of her suit.

Typical.

He must be a god.

But not one she'd met before; he couldn't possibly be human looking that good.

She recovered herself enough to mumble, "thank you," and shuffled a little further away from the scent of hot clean body that she really shouldn't have been able to appreciate in that wind.

And yet, it was as if he carried a tiny cloud of stillness with him, that left him completely unaffected by the troubles of ordinary men.

Another reason to label him a god and back away while she could.

"You should be careful," he said, "texting while you walk is never a good idea."

The traffic lights sounded don't walk.

"Of course. I'm sorry to trouble you," she risked looking up at him as a large truck barrelled around the corner.

And heard the sickening sound of a phone being ground beneath three double sets of tyres.

Her face paled and she clenched and unclenched her left hand - the emptiness told her it was *her* phone in pieces on its way down the street.

And her life with it.

Not that it was that hard to get a new phone, but it might be years before she managed to get a new one set up with universal roaming and all her favourite apps.

Especially the ones she couldn't remember the passwords for.

And the ones she used to keep herself occupied when her sisters were quarrelling.

She closed her eyes and started enunciating as many swearwords as she could think of.

Quietly, in her mind, less the god thought she was common.

"I'm so sorry," he said, "I didn't mean for you to use your phone. Let me buy you a new one."

She sighed; partly from sorrow, and partly because she feared for her sanity should she spend any more time with him than she had to.

"No thanks, it's my fault. I'm just thankful it was my phone and not me under that truck."

"I insist."

"No really, it's fine."

The traffic lights signalled walk again, "I must go," she said, "I can't be late back to work as well."

And with that lie, she ran down the street as fast as her pencil skirt and stilettos would let her.

Slowing down as she ducked through an arcade, down some stairs, and into the dark, beery scented recesses of her favourite wine bar.

After that embarrassment, she *needed* several very large, very strong alcoholic drinks.

The bar was the place she spent most of her time, and she tended to think of it as her office.

After all, she was there most of the day, and well into the evening.

It seemed easier and less stressful to get things done than at home.

Which was almost fair enough because as well as more cluttered than she could stand, her home also contained her sisters.

Whereas the bar was blissfully free of both sisters and clutter.

If she hadn't needed her sisters as much as they needed her, she would have moved out.

Come to think of it, these days they spent a lot of time apart.

Wouldn't it be more practical for them to share an apartment building than a house?

Then they could all get a bit of space when they needed to get away from each other.

It was just not possible she was the only sister who got annoyed by their constant close proximity.

Then again, so far as she knew, none of them knew how far they could get from each other.

Or for how long.

She smiled at the barman as she walked in, and he asked, "the usual?"

Laura nodded on her way through to her favourite table; the one in a small alcove where she could sit with her back to the wall, and her face towards the door.

The lights were a little dim, which gave her a sense of privacy.

The wooden floors could have made the space echo, but the plush chairs and curtains around the walls absorbed much of the noise.

Most of the patrons were middle-ageish, and most just wanted somewhere for a quiet drink, so the sound of conversation was muted.

While she waited for her Negroni and charcuterie plate, she slipped her shoes off, ignoring how difficult they would be to get them back on.

Then wriggled her toes and flexed her ankles.

At the same time, she took a deep breath and held it while she rocked her head back and forth across her shoulders, then rotated each shoulder back opening up the sockets.

When she felt slightly less stressed, she started looking for her backup device.

Also known as The Notebook, complete with a slim black and silver fountain pen attached to the cover with an elastic band.

Without the phone, those who wanted her would be drawn to the bar, and she'd need the book to record their wishes in.

It was never a conscious choice to open for business, (so to speak), but that people just started arriving when she was ready for them.

And whatever the reason, they just told her their life stories.

Laura laid her notebook on the table before her, opened up to a new blank page, and tucked the fountain pen between the pages to mark her place.

From her position, there were several tables between her and the door, which allowed her the opportunity to observe punters as they came in.

They were generally recognisable by the way they meandered through the bar, always stopping for a quick shot of liquid courage on their way.

She took a sip of her drink and speared a piece of bresaola, as she watched a man approach.

She didn't actually listen to what he said, but observed what she saw.

In the old days she'd look through clients to the weave of their threads. The weft showed where they'd been and were headed, and the warp the obstacles in their path. And when she'd seen the lay of the weave, she'd twitch it.

But it took them years to come and go, and by the time they'd got to her, the cloth would have sorted itself out.

As time went by, they moved a little faster, taking only months to find her.

They'd stopped thinking of themselves as tapestries and started thinking of themselves as books.

She learned to read them, editing the details to change their endings.

Modern life, by comparison, was exhaustingly instant, and modern people thought of themselves as movies. She'd taught herself to scroll through their lives, editing, erasing, or sometimes allowing a second take.

But more people wanted more dramatic edits, and they wanted them more often.

To distract the time-wasters she'd seeded ideas through the universes. The quick fixes offered by magazines and influencers took some of the load, leaving her free to focus on the complex issues.

Which it had to be said, were generally more interesting.

The man, seemingly satisfied, left. She noted the details so she'd remember them to pass them onto her sister Agatha.

Not that it mattered, Agatha could see the future while Laura only saw the present.

A woman was next, then another man, and another.

And after a while, she lost track of how many there were.

Laura sighed, closed her eyes, and rotated her head on her shoulders again.

It was time to call it a day.

She was tired, grumpy about the phone, and wanted to relax in a hot bath.

Just one more client...

Then she'd call it a day.

She could read this guy with her eyes closed; drinks, dinner, leading to marriage, kids, hand-holding in old age.

Laura found the woman he was thinking about weirdly familiar.

And there was something about his cologne.

She opened her eyes and found herself looking into the green eyes of the guy who'd put her back on her feet that morning.

He said nothing, just looked at her.

Judging her?

Or her reaction to him.

Hard to say with that inscrutable face.

She thought about what he'd probably seen.

A bunch of people coming to her table one by one, stopping for a short time, then leaving while she made notes in The Notebook.

And as she laid down her pen, the next person arrived.

Was he thinking bookmaking?

Drugs?

Prostitution?

For a moment she fretted about what he thought she'd been up to.

And then she realised it was none of his bloody business.

She frowned.

"That's my girl," he said and leant forward to lay a hand on hers.

Instantly, they were standing halfway up a mountain somewhere.

Definitely a god then.

A god with nothing better to do with his time than spend it bugging her.

A god who looked insanely attractive in jeans and a tight green sweater that matched his eyes.

She sucked in a breath of crisp clear air and looked around her.

The sun shone in a clear sky; a little off centre, so sometime late morning or early afternoon.

The dark grey rocky slope beneath her suggested volcano (hopefully extinct), and she looked up to see snow on the peaks; seemingly close enough to walk to.

A gentle breeze caressed her hair, and when she reached up to smooth it back, she realised she was wearing blue jeans and a red plaid flannel button-down shirt.

She shuddered with discomfort at the garish outfit.

Now that she'd seen it, she couldn't not see it, and soon it seemed that all she could see was a red plaid flannel pillow encompassing the world.

She couldn't think with all that noise going on.

A gust of wind set her hair flying, and when she tried to get it back under control, she realised it was longer than before.

The bloody cheek of him.

She patted her pockets and found nothing in them.

A quick glance at her feet revealed chestnut coloured hiking boots, but no bag, and no Notebook.

Had he perhaps *deliberately* thrown her phone under the truck?

For a moment she panicked, then remembered that her sister Claudia saw the past, and with Agatha seeing the future, they should be able to track her down soon enough.

"Why would you want your sisters to track you?" he asked. "Haven't you wanted to get away from them for centuries?"

She folded arms and glared at him.

He shrugged, "I think you should leap at the chance to lead that ordinary life you've been thinking about."

"I don't see much ordinary about shacking up with a god who's got tickets on himself," she snapped.

If it wasn't bad enough that he'd changed her clothes and messed with her hair, now he was telling her what to do?

He laughed, "I could do with a hot chocolate, how about you?" He grabbed her hand and started walking down the mountain towards what looked like a ski lift station.

She tried to pull her hand free with little success.

And wondered very quietly, could he really read her mind?

Or was he predicting her reaction based on what he knew about her?

And how long exactly had he known about her while she had no notion about him?

Stalker much?

He knew she had sisters, but did he know who they were?

Or regardless of how much they detested each other in any given moment, how much they needed each other?

Still trying to detach her hand, but this time to help maintain her balance, she followed him into the station café.

Obviously, they were the only ones in the place. Not even anyone behind the counter.

Was it possible he could stop time?

He went behind the espresso machine to froth milk and pour it over some shaved chocolate in large ceramic mugs.

Thought he was so bloody smart.

It would take more than a man who knew his way around a coffee machine to impress her.

She wandered into the kitchen, trying not to arouse his suspicion, and finding a large kitchen knife she used it to hack her hair into a ragged bob.

Leaving the excess on the floor, she wandered back to the main café.

Only this time she walked into a wall of noise produced by one hundred hyperactive children. "Mummy, mummy," they shouted and latched onto her legs, and she counted them at five.

Five children somewhere between the ages of five and ten.

Or given the way god children aged, anywhere between five and five hundred.

Five children who laughed as they reached back to grab her the minute she prised them off her.

She turned to see where the god was, and he was sitting in an overstuffed armchair in a lounge room.

"What the ffff...," even though these were not really children, she tried to think of a clean word to use.

"What the fudge?"

"Isn't this what you wanted? A home of your own, a husband and children?"

"Not all on the same day!"

She rocked on her feet as the children disappeared.

"And not like this," she continued, flinging her right arm up to encompass him and his armchair, "but the old-fashioned way. The way humans do it. Meeting. Dating. Gifts. Falling in love."

"Are you sure? Sounds tedious."

She sank into herself, "I'm sure."

The room disappeared, and she was sitting at her table in the bar again. Trying to work out what had just happened.

But the more desperately she tried to remember it, the more quickly it slipped away.

«« • »»

She sighed, closed her eyes, and rotated her head on her shoulders.

It was time to call it a day.

She was tired, grumpy about the phone, and wanted to relax in a hot bath.

Just one more client...

Then she'd call it a day.

She could read this guy with her eyes closed; drinks, dinner, leading to marriage, kids, hand-holding in old age.

His cologne was fresh and citrusy. There was something familiar about it.

She opened her eyes and found herself look-ing into the green eyes of the guy who'd put her back on her feet that morning.

"Oh," she said.

"I wasn't sure it was you, but I thought I'd stop by and see."

"It's me all right," she closed The Notebook, slipping the pen into its elastic and put it in her bag.

He put a small box on the table, "I felt really bad about your phone so I got you another one."

Laura rested her hands on the table but didn't touch the box.

"How did you know I would be here?"

"I didn't. I just dropped in here for a drink be-fore heading home. It must be Fate."

She managed not to roll her eyes at the corny chat up line.

He nudged the box closer to her, "please take it."

She sighed and reached out for the box, "thank you?"

"Eurus, my name's Eurus."

Definitely a god then, and still using his true name.

"Laura." He might know hers, but she and her sisters had agreed to go incognito.

"Can I get you another drink Laura?" He glanced at his watch, "or seeing as it's getting late, maybe some dinner?"

She should go home, but the evening had just got interesting. She threw the box in her bag, "why not? Let's get out of here."

THE END

AUTHOR OF THE HISTORIES OF HAYWARD HALL
ALEXANDRIA
BLAELOCK
CHARGING
INTO FATE
A SHORT STORY

CHARGING INTO FATE

"Last bookshop 1,000 km." Marguerite read the sign aloud as it flashed past.

"That's funny isn't it? That should really read last servo."

"Hmmm?" said Steve.

"Last bookshop."

"Yeah, right," he mustered up a chuckle though she could see his mind wasn't really on it.

She sighed and looked out the window again.

Miles and miles of flat, black, bushfire scarred land; scrub bushes regrowing low on the ground with the odd burnt out tree trunk standing like a dark statue from a long-ago civilisation.

As they flashed past another trunk, she thought it looked like a man fallen to his knees with his hands thrown up.

She whispered, "My name is Ozymandias, King of Kings," out the window, quoting Percy Bysshe Shelley.

Not spoken out loud, because she knew Steve was not a big fan of poetry.

He thought she was being uppity, flaunting her middle-class upbringing before him. Showing off.

She watched Ozymandias recede into the distance with the side mirror and corrected herself.

Miles and miles *and* miles of burnt-out bush.

It made her heart ache, though she couldn't say what for.

The creatures that once lived there?

The extent of the devastation?

Or that it reminded her of her own life.

Trashed and burned, an empty wasteland of neglected and forgotten dreams. And she was fairly sure it was all because of Steve.

Well, not all Steve, obviously she had a hand in it too.

But somewhere along the line, she'd forgotten who she was.

And a crap tonne of show-offy poetry.

She knew Steve was planning to dump her. And given he'd blown through all her savings; it was only a matter of time.

Weeks if not days.

He probably had a new mark, primed and ready to go.

She knew exactly how it would happen.

One day he'd just move in with the next girl and disappear, leaving her to deal with the fall-out; probably superannuation funds stripped bare, loans and credit cards she didn't know she'd taken out, and overly aggressive debt collectors.

But that was okay.

The day after that, she'd start picking up the pieces, and she'd be glad.

Marguerite vowed she would never allow herself to blindly trust someone like that again.

Weird though that he wanted one last holiday. A trip along the Coral Coast; Perth, Geraldton, Shark Bay, Carnarvon, Exmouth.

Staying at the Cape Range National Park, to look at the gorges and the reef, and then coming home

Aside from being with Steve 24/7, she was having a good time.

Idly she wondered what the last bookshop would be like.

She imagined something like an old wood cabin, half falling down, the boards scoured clean of paint by the strong coastal winds.

Perhaps there was a single petrol bowser out the front, one of those old manual ones that had dinged as the thingy turned in a globe so you could see and hear the petrol pumping.

And they'd have a café, half full of junk with a table or two, selling dry, old pies a week or two old.

More likely it would be someone's idea of a joke - no one read books any more.

They'd do better selling handicrafts. Allegedly made by natives like they did in America.

Steve slowed the car as he approached a fork in the road.

In the middle of the fork sat a roadhouse.

An oddly charming, more or less modern, red brick construction with a well-maintained parking lot and a grassy area with gas barbecues and pic-nic settings.

It was fascinatingly at odds with the burnt-out bush surrounding it, and she wanted to go in and check it out, but Steve drove right by it, as if it didn't exist.

If nothing else, she'd have welcomed a decent shower given they'd been camping for a few days without running water.

She opened her mouth to ask to go back, but as she turned towards him, she saw his jaw tense and decided not.

He'd just ruin it for her anyway.

Maybe on the way back.

After all, they might know a bit more about the Last Bookshop.

Steve drove right through to the village, and then a little further to a parking lot almost on the beach.

Marguerite got out of the car and stretched. The burned-out bush gave way to a stretch of white sandy beach and blue green sea, with actual fish in it, took her breath away.

Absolutely stunning.

She clawed her long hair back from her face, and swept it back up into a pony tail. Freeing her sweaty neck to catch the drying seaweed scented breeze off the ocean.

And a sprinkling of beach sand as well.

Steve was the beachy one of the pair, while she preferred the bush. But aside from the sun-burn she was getting, she was glad to be there; somewhere away from the ordinary.

Something about the sun coming at her from all directions was refreshing and invigorating, rather than being shaded by office blocks as she was all day at work.

Or under the shifting shadows of the trees in her garden at home.

Someone nearby laughed, for a moment louder than the seagulls begging for hot chips.

You'd think they'd be bored of chips, wanting something different for a change.

"Go get some cold drinks and I'll see if there's a room at the hotel," he said.

She nodded and wandered down the street, looking in the windows for drinks.

Next to no time later, someone grabbed her arm firmly; her head whipped round, saw it was Steve carrying the look of thunder.

Reflexively, she looked at her watch to see if she'd taken too long.

"Stupid hotel has no rooms. We have to back up down the highway, somewhere called the Palace Hotel."

"Oh, we passed it on the way in."

"Did we? I didn't see it."

Marguerite couldn't imagine how he'd missed it given its size, but he was clearly irritated, so she didn't say anything.

Now wasn't the time to be getting "uppity" as he called it.

She took the safe way out and grunted; he could interpret that anyway that took his fancy.

"Let's go," he said, and started dragging her back up the street.

By the arm.

Not transferring his grip to her hand.

"You don't want to see what's here before we leave?" she asked, a little bit sulkily because they had after all just arrived.

"Nah, it's late. Let's go."

Marguerite wanted to look at her watch again, because she was pretty sure it wasn't that late.

Though the evenings seemed to stretch out like full days themselves, and the night fell suddenly.

But she meekly followed him back to the car.

It wasn't worth getting into an argument about that.

Steve had no trouble finding the Palace Hotel this time.

He barely slowed at the entrance and arrived in the central parking lot with a squeal of tires.

He slammed the car door, and stamped his way up the stairs and into the hotel.

With more time to look at it, she could see two arms running down each leg of the Y.

One with petrol bowsers, and the other a small hotel complex; its faded sign reading Palace Hotel.

A café in the centre, with a small general and souvenir store with an enclosed outdoor.

Through elaborate ironwork gates, she could see an enclosed outdoor eating area with a sign declaring it dog-friendly.

Marguerite stopped to pat the ageing Labrador sunning itself on the verandah.

As she waked inside, she was surprised to see a kind of mid-century modern reception area. A sort of glassed-in sun room, conservatory thing with terrazzo floors.

A young red-headed woman standing at the polished red wood reception desk was smiling politely and just starting her spiel.

"Welcome to the Palace Hotel, my name's Diana. How can I help you today?"

"Room please," Steve snapped.

Marguerite could see he'd about reached his limit, and crossed her fingers that poor Diana would speed up and get the conversation over and done with before he exploded.

She sat on the edge of a nearby slim, wood framed chair, preparing herself to intervene if necessary.

The dog from the verandah wandered inside and sat beside her, putting his head in her lap.

She looked down at it and started scratching his head. It cocked his head to give her better access behind its ears.

She wasn't sure exactly what happened next, but suddenly Diana was kneeling before her saying, "excuse me, are you okay?"

She jumped and sat bolt upright, which startled the dog enough to stand up and back away a few paces, then she craned her neck looking left and right for Steve.

"It's okay, I sent him to the bar with a free coupon."

"Oh. I... The room. I."

Diana smiled, and rested a hand on Marguerite's arm, "are you okay?"

"I." She took a deep breath and tried again, "I'm fine, thanks for asking."

Diana looked at Marguerite's lap where her fingers were tightly woven together.

"I'm not sure that's entirely true, is it?"

Marguerite looked into Diana's soft brown eyes and went as still as a rabbit caught in head-lights.

"He hasn't treated you well, has he?"

Marguerite didn't say a word.

"Your Spidey senses are telling you something's not quite right, aren't they?"

Even if she could've broken eye contact with Diana, Marguerite couldn't have said anything.

Even if she'd wanted to.

Diana tucked a fallen lock of hair behind Marguerite's ear to better see her face, and said "it's not safe for you here with him, is it?"

Marguerite managed to swallow and look away.

"Wouldn't you like to visit the bookshop?"

After a long pause, in which Diana said nothing, Marguerite spoke as of she was in a dream. "I would actually. I meant to ask you about that."

She snapped back into the room, "wait. What do you mean I'm not safe?"

Diana sat back on her heels, "there's just something about a hunter only another hunter can see."

Marguerite looked at the dog, and it looked back at her.

It was true.

She'd been walking on eggshells since they'd left, trying not to upset him.

Trying not to give him an excuse.

An excuse to...

She *really* wasn't safe.

But.

She didn't know what to do about it.

And she didn't think she had the strength to do anything, even if she knew what the best thing to actually do was.

"Why don't you visit the bookshop? I'm sure that will help clear your mind."

"I couldn't possibly drive Steve's car without his permission."

"So? Take mine."

"I really couldn't."

"You really could."

Diana got up, revealing her feet were bare, and walked behind the reception counter, coming back with a set of keys she threw at Marguerite, "it's the red Valiant Charger in the parking lot."

Marguerite caught the keys, then twisted her body to look into the lot, and then back at the woman.

"That's *your* muscle car?"

She put her hands on her hips, seemingly amused by Marguerite's reaction, "sure is."

"But you seem..." she blushed and dropped her head.

Diana laughed, "looks can be deceiving."

Marguerite grinned, "if you loan me that car I might never come back."

"Don't worry about the car, she *always* finds her way back."

Marguerite weighed the keys in her hand.

Aware that Steve wouldn't be happy when he found out she'd gone out on her own.

Getting in Diana's car and driving away would change her one way or another.

"Won't the shop be shut by now?"

"I can give them a call and ask them to wait for you."

She looked at the keys; old and worn as they were.

On the cusp of a seemingly small and insignificant decision, she felt as though the universe was holding its breath to see what she might do.

She looked up at Diana's knowing gaze, seeing something older and wiser than the woman appeared to be.

"Yes. Okay then, yes.

"I'll visit the bookshop."

"Perfect," Diana said, "turn left as you leave the hotel - it's closer than you think. Just let them know I sent you."

Marguerite walked out the door, got in the car and turned the key before she could change her mind.

And before Steve could catch her.

The car roared into life with a loud enough rumble of thunder to call the dead back to life.

Certainly loud enough to startle a flock of cockatoos into life, squawking their dismay as they launched from the trees into the air.

Marguerite slowly backed out of the parking bay, feeling as though the car wanted to drive more than she did.

Turning left, letting it rip, and rocketing up the highway.

But you can't cruise without tunes, so she turned the radio on and randomly pushed a button to tune it.

The sound of Jet blasted from the concealed speakers, "Bring it on Back", if she remembered correctly. One of her favourites.

It was on the jukebox when she'd first met Steve.

Thirty seconds earlier, or thirty seconds later and she'd have missed him.

Gone for that other guy, what was his name?

The cute one.

So appropriate for the situation she found herself in at that moment.

She belted out the song.

And then, suddenly, the bookshop leapt into being on the highway as she approached it.

Or at least it was probably the bookshop though it looked more like a house.

She pulled in, parked a little way from both the road and the shop, and turned off the engine.

With the throbbing engine silenced, it was so quiet she was convinced she could hear electricity crackling in the air.

The shop was almost exactly as she imagined it.

An old weatherboard building, the sun setting behind it, possibly held together by dead termite nests, its white paint peeling to reveal weathered grey boards.

No petrol bowsers, and no café.

Three women sat on Adirondack chairs arranged in a curve under an awning stretching out from the roof. They shared a round table, on which sat a wine bottle and four glasses, three of them half full.

The woman closest to her was twenty-ish, wearing tight red jeans and t-shirt. A strawberry blonde plait hung down one shoulder.

She was sitting cross legged, and appeared to be knitting, but what was dropping from her nee-dles was more like a tangled ball of different threads than something coherent like a beanie or maybe a cardigan.

The woman in the middle looked fortyish, and sprawled in her seat, legs and feet akimbo. She was wearing a black skirt and open-collared shirt, fanning herself with a black fan.

Her black hair was caught up on her head with something like a chopstick, exposing the back of her neck to what passed as a cool breeze.

There was an empty chair between her and an ageless woman with short white hair, and a long white dress.

She sat upright, one leg slung across the other, gently swaying in time to a tune Marguerite could almost hear.

She held a pair of scissors in her hand, and was using one blade to trim splinters from the table.

Marguerite shook herself and got out of the car.

Not exactly sure what to expect, though the scene before her made her think more of an outdoor wine bar than a bookshop.

All they needed was a fire pit to make it more like a beach barbecue.

She walked towards the women, "Um. Hi. Diana sent me?"

"Would you care to join us for some wine?" the white-haired woman asked.

Marguerite found herself wanting a glass of wine more than anything else in the world. "That would be lovely if you have one to spare."

The black-haired woman patted the empty seat beside her. Marguerite sat down, allowed the blonde to pour her a glass of Rosé.

"Cheers," she said, raising her glass to the women, who raised theirs and they drank together.

"Oh, that's lovely," Marguerite said, her face brightening, "it makes me think of one Summer when I was about fifteen and the carnival came to town. I fell madly in love with a handsome brown eyed boy who worked the dodgem cars."

She smiled fondly as she looked back.

"How could I have forgotten about him? What was his name?" She looked up into the sky trying to remember.

"Something exotic. I can picture him now, and on my god, he was so beautiful. I went back every day for the week to see him."

The blonde smiled at her, "how did it turn out?"

Marguerite's face fell. "Ah. He moved away when the carnival closed, and I never saw him again. But before he left, he gave me my first kiss - he was such a good kisser."

Marguerite smiled for a moment at the memory, and then looked at the blonde woman, "I sometimes wonder what happened to him, and who he married, and whether he's happy."

"Ah, your first love. What do you think happened?" the black-haired woman asked, and Marguerite laughed.

"I'd like to think he still pines for me even now, but I actually hope that wherever he is, he's happy. With a job he loves, a wife he adores, and a life that makes him happy."

She took another sip of her wine as the black- and white-haired women looked at each other. The black raised an eyebrow, and the white shook her head a little.

Marguerite took another sip of wine, and said, "it's funny how life turns out, isn't it?"

"Yes," the dark-haired woman replied.

"Goodness," said Marguerite, "how rude of me! My name's Marguerite."

The women went round the circle, saying their names.

"Claudia," said the blond.

"Laura," the black-haired woman.

"Agatha," the white-haired.

"I'm very pleased to meet you," said Marguerite.

And she really was, but couldn't have said why. Maybe because she was just relaxing as the wine took effect.

"And what's your current boyfriend like?" asked Laura, "is he nice? Does he make your heart race like your first love?"

"Chalk and cheese," Marguerite drained the glass, "to be honest, I think he's going to dump me."

She looked into her empty glass, and Claudia filled it up again.

"But I don't care; I wish he was dead," she drank some more.

"Actually no, I don't wish he was dead. And I don't really wish I'd never met him. He was so sweet in the beginning. I..." she waved her hands around, sloshing a little of the wine from the glass and over her hands.

She put the glass down and licked it from her hands and fingers.

"You what?" asked Agatha.

"I wish I hadn't been naive enough, or maybe foolish enough to get in so deep so quickly. That when he tried to move in, I'd said no. That when he asked for money, I'd said no. That I was a stronger person. Less desperate for love."

"Wish you'd met the boy at the carnival again?" asked Laura.

"Maybe. When your first is so blissful, I think it sets you up to be a loser in love forever."

"I expect that's all the fairy tales we hear when we're children," said Claudia.

"So cynical for one so young," said Agatha,

"Do you think there's one true love for everyone then?" asked Laura.

"I used to," Marguerite reached for the glass, and Claudia filled it up again. "Now I think love is more of a love for right now thing. Maybe you're lucky and you grow at the same pace, but more likely one of you changes more than the other and you break apart."

"Some people never change," said Agatha, "some people never grow up or move on."

"Like Steve. He's like a perpetual child, and when he uses up one woman, he discards them and moves onto the next."

"Are you sure he moves on," asked Claudia, "have you ever met any of his past girlfriends?"

"Ummmmmm. No, I don't think I have," Marguerite yawned widely, extending her neck to put her face in the air.

"And did you ask him why he wanted to take a trip with you right now?" asked Laura.

Marguerite rested her elbow on the table, and leaned her head on it. "Um, no. I thought it was just a last goodbye. Why do you ask?" she yawned again.

"Did you consider that maybe he doesn't plan to break up with you? Maybe he wants to kill you?" asked Agatha.

"That's very dark…" Marguerite mumbled, "why on earth would you ask that?"

She started snoring.

The following morning, she woke alone with a slight hangover which she put down to drinking without eating.

And the remains of a dream about three women and a bookshop. Who'd changed her life somehow.

She took a long hot shower, washing the grease of several days camping from her body and her hair.

As she looked in the mirror to comb her hair, something was bugging her, but her head hurt, and she was so agitated she couldn't quite put her finger on it.

She took some clean clothes out of the drawer, fairly sure she hadn't unpacked, and all her clothes needed washing.

There was no sign of Steve, his bag hadn't been touched, but the car was not in the lot where he'd left it.

For a moment she panicked, thinking he'd abandoned her, then remembered his bag hadn't been disturbed.

Besides, when she was looking at the route, she recalled seeing reference to a coach line.

If the worse came to the worst, there was always a bus.

Even with the car, there was no point looking
for him, no doubt he'd turn up. Annoyed about
something or another.

At the café she ordered a strong latte and sat on
the verandah to drink it.

It was still Summer, but the morning air had a
chill in it, so she dragged a chair into the morning
sun.

She couldn't be bothered going back to the
room for something warmer, so while her back
warmed up, she still shivered a little with the cold
in her front.

The hotel dog wandered by, then came back
and sat leaning on her leg, sniffing up at her as
she bent to scratch its head.

She saw a police car driving up the highway,
and as she watched it turned in and parked.

After a moment, a tall dark-haired guy got out.
He put his hat on, she guessed to signal that this
visit was for business, and started walking towards the hotel.

The dog fidgeted, and he turned his head towards her as he walked. Registering her presence,
he touched his hat and she nodded in acknowl-

edgement as he walked up the steps and into the hotel.

A short while later, Diana brought him outside and introduced him to her, "Marguerite, this is Senior Sargent Victor Moreno, and he—."

The Police Officer put his hand on Diana's arm to stop her saying anything further.

"I'm making enquiries about the last known movements of," he took a notebook from his breast pocket, flipped it open and after consulting is, "Gerald McEvoy."

Marguerite gaped at him.

"I don't know any Gerald McEvoy!"

"Yet you checked in with him yesterday evening."

"I checked in with Steve Lewis."

He glanced at Diana, wrote something in his notebook, then asked Marguerite, "what is the nature of your relationship with this Steve Lewis?"

"He's my boyfriend."

"And have you been dating long?"

"Only feels that way."

He raised an eyebrow at her, "I don't know, couple of months? Six months tops."

"And where were you last night?"

"She was in the bar 'til late," Diana said.

He frowned at her.

"I'm just saying. She was very drunk, and probably doesn't remember. We took her back to her room at about 2 am."

He rubbed his eyebrows, "your license to serve alcohol expires at midnight."

"As you well know, we stop serving alcohol at midnight. But being a Roadhouse, the premises are open 24 hours a day for food and other beverages."

He sighed, "let's see the tape then."

Curious, Marguerite tagged along.

They all crowded into the manager's office, even the dog.

Diana sat at the desk and queued the playback on her laptop. They watched the replay, a little clock in the top left-hand corner running through the time.

It started just before she and Steve walked in. Her recollection of the evening was quite different, but she didn't say anything.

Diana paused the playback to show Steve leaving at about eight, and he made a note in his book.

Marguerite was fascinated by the footage of her eating and drinking, talking to people she didn't recognise, and then falling asleep at the table.

And after a while, Diana and another woman picked her up and took her out.

Diana slid the mouse and queued footage of the car park. Steve walked out, got in the car, and drove off. The playback continued as Diana explained, "the room was empty when we got her into it, and the bed hadn't been slept in."

A few trucks came and went, but right up until that moment, there was no sign of Steve.

"So what's this about?" Marguerite asked.

"I regret to inform you that the body of Gerald McEvoy, or as you know him, Steven Lewis was discovered this morning."

Marguerite sat down, but with no chair to catch her, she fell to the floor.

Unable to get a grip on her emotions.

Unsure whether to laugh or cry.

Fully aware that Senior Sargent Victor Moreno was there to witness everything.

She felt bad for wishing him dead.

Because despite what Diana's video had shown, she knew she'd driven off in her red charger to find the bookshop.

Skipping out on Steve, and not worrying about him in the slightest.

"I think she's gone into shock," Diana told the Senior Sargent, "perhaps it would be best if you came back later?"

He seemed reluctant to leave, but eventually nodded and left.

Diana helped her up.

"I wished he was dead."

"Wishes don't create reality. Come and get another coffee."

Marguerite looked at her.

She shrugged and pulled Marguerite through to the café, "not that kind of reality anyway.

"According to Moreno, hikers found his remains some way off the highway. They think he was attacked by wild dogs."

"But when I was at the bookshop, I wished he was dead. What if they say something?"

Diana went behind the espresso machine and started making two coffees, "they won't say anything to the Police because the bookshop is the kind of place that only appears when someone needs it."

"And you said wishes don't change reality."

"Maybe it wasn't your wish? Did you consider that?"

Marguerite gave her a blank look.

Diana hesitated, and something in Marguerite's made up her mind, "maybe all the other women he brought here finally got their re-venge."

"What do you mean all the other women?"

Diana smiled grimly and handed her a coffee.

After sipping her own she said, "you're not the only one he's brought through here. One every few months for the last few years."

Marguerite's face paled, "how did he explain that?"

"Sisters, cousins, girlfriends."

"What do you think happened then?"

"I think in a few days, they're going to start digging up dead women."

And that was exactly as much cold hard reality as Marguerite could deal with at that moment.

"I think I need to go back to bed and wake up this morning again."

"Sleep well."

Back in her room, fully made up despite the early hour and the mess she'd left behind, she curled up on her side and pulled the bedspread over herself.

There had to be more going on here than met the eye.

Three women running a bookshop that was only there when you needed it. Claudia... Clotho? Knitting something that looked messed up and tangled. Like her life if she was honest.

"Diana" running a hotel.

Steve torn apart by wild dogs.

Yes, she'd wished him dead, and suddenly, maybe magically, she was free of him.

And then she remembered the thing that was bugging her, and went back to the bathroom to check it.

She had a hazy memory of cutting her hair at the bookshop, and sure enough it was several inches shorter.

And she hadn't over-soaped it, like you normally do when you cut your hair. Nor had Diana mentioned it to her.

But the dog had seemed to know something was different about her.

What bargain exactly had she struck for her hair? She had to find out.

She walked over to the charger, and she looked around to see if anyone was watching before opening the door. The keys were still in the ignition, and shortly after that, she was turning left and zooming along the highway.

An hour later, she was approaching the next town and still hadn't seen the bookshop.

She was tempted to keep going, but was sure she hadn't made it this far the day before.

In any case, she didn't really *need* the bookshop. Assuming she had before.

Shouldn't they have given her a contract?

No, that was deals with the devil.

Regretfully, she turned the car around and headed back.

She hadn't even got a book!

Diana was leaning on a verandah post when she got back.

"You're not going to tell me?"

"I don't know the details. They are a law unto themselves; even I'm not immune to their powers, so I don't ever push them."

"But what did they do?"

"All I can tell you is that now and again I do them a favour, and then again and now, I just steer someone who needs them their way."

"Like maybe you go hunting?"

She let the silence grow.

And then she pulled a book from behind her back and held it out, "they asked me to give you this."

Marguerite took the book and walked past Diana, taking the book and walking through to the bar.

"Vodka tonic," she told the barman. When the drink was ready, she paid and took it to a seat in the window.

She plunked the book face down on the table, arranged so all she could see were the edges of the pages. The old pages. And the beautifully tooled, possibly leather cover.

What, she wondered, was she supposed to tell the Police Officer when he came back.

For that matter, what was she supposed to do with the rest of her life?

She took a sip of her drink, then dragged the book towards her, turned it over and opened the cover.

The front page was empty.

She turned the page, and that was empty too.

Picking it up, she flicked through all the pages, and they were all empty.

Marguerite turned back to the front, and flipped the first page again. As she looked, a picture emerged from the page.

It looked like a party photo of grinning women, but more like the kind of painting you see as a frontispiece in an old book.

She was about to slam the cover shut, but the woman brandishing a fist full of hair caught her eye; it was her. With Claudia, Laura and Agatha surrounding her.

And then some faded, spidery handwriting came into focus on what would otherwise be the title page.

Your fate is unwritten,

Here's to making your own destiny.

Suddenly starving, she flagged a waitress down for a menu, and a few moments later, ordered a country meat pie with vegetables and mash.

Someone stood next to the table, "may I join you?" Senior Sargent Victor Moreno asked.

She shrugged.

He sat opposite her, took his hat off and sat it on the chair between them.

"This is a bit off-topic, but I feel like I've met you before."

"I don't think so. I'm not sure I've ever met anyone called Victor Moreno."

"Ah, my parents died in an accident when I was young and I went to live with my aunt and uncle. When they adopted me, they changed my name so I wouldn't always be reminded of them."

"Oh, that's... sweet. I guess.

"I don't come from here; I grew up in rural Victoria.

"My parents were carnies, and they travelled a rural circuit through Victoria?"

Marguerite thought about her conversation with at the bookshop. "Traralgon?"

"Wait," he fumbled for his wallet, and pulled a set of photo booth picture out, old and worn where generations of wallets had creased them.

"You have to be kidding me," said Margeurite.

"No, really. Is this you?"

And of course he was the boy from the summer carnival.

If you'd got as far as a bookshop that wasn't there, and a book waiting to be written, who else could he possibly be.

Though she had to admit to herself, if not to him, that she was happy to meet him again.

Though she wondered, just a little bit, whether he'd always been there, or they'd pulled him from somewhere else for her.

"To be honest," he said, "this puts me in a bit of a bind."

"Yes?"

"Well, I came to tell you not to leave the area until our enquiries have finished, but there was something about your silhouette in the window."

"I see. You want to get to know me, but you can't until you've cleared me as a suspect. Presumably until the case is closed."

"Ah, yeah. Though it just got complicated. You see, we found human remains in the bush near where Gerald McEvoy parked his car."

"So, it might take some time," she struggled to repress a smile.

"Yes."

"Well, I have a couple of weeks leave from work, and it seems I don't have any plans as such..."

"Oh, well that's great. I mean fortunate. For the investigation."

She sipped her drink, "indeed it is."

THE END

AUTHOR OF THE HISTORIES OF HAYWARD HALL
ALEXANDRIA BLAELOCK
EMBRACING FATE
A SHORT STORY

EMBRACING FATE

When Susan Grant died, Agatha was there; right next to the bed.

Susan was stuck in the air-conditioned hospice room, slipping in and out of consciousness.

Agatha knew she was aware of the cold, and the familiar smells of antiseptic and the chemicals they used to clean the machines.

Though she may not have been fully aware of the full extent of the room's greyness; grey lino on the floor, grey paint on the walls, and grey laminated cupboards on the walls.

Even some kind of weird grey on grey abstract painting on the wall facing the bed.

Agatha wondered if the greyness was sup-posed to ease the transition between life and death, though anyone who wasn't dying when they came in would certainly be when they walked out.

In fact, everyone was dying.

Day by day drawing closer to their deaths.

Except her of course, given she controlled the date and means of everyone's death.

Agatha put her tiny posy of pale blue forget-me-nots in a plastic cup from the water dispenser in the grey waiting room and arranged them on top of the grey cupboard.

She put her shapeless bag on the grey vinyl covered foam padded chair beside the bed, and not wanting to be bothered with overly cheerful bustling nurses, shut the door.

The grey curtains around the bed were closed, as were the room dividing curtains and the windows curtains.

Way too much grey.

Susan's poor, emaciated, corpse like body, clad in a grey hospital gown, was a mass of cheery red, blue and green wires and tubes hooked up to beeping machines.

This, Agatha knew, was not the way Susan had wanted to go.

Susan had looked forward to dying naturally.

Ideally on a park bench in some lovely gardens; tall gum trees, riotous flowers, and lots of bright chirping parrots.

Perhaps somewhere near a lake or river.

Somewhere tranquil and relaxing where she could lay her earthly worries aside before calmly moving on to whatever happened next.

Too late for that now.

"I'll just open up the windows and let some air in here shall I?" asked Agatha as she pulled back the curtains, and opened the window as wide as it would go to let the sunshine and clean fresh smell of warm eucalyptus into the room.

"You're not any better I see," she said as she ferreted out a couple of coins and laid them one at a time on Susan's eyelids, then sat next to the bed.

Susan of course said nothing, but Agatha took her hand and put herself in Susan's memory, which was about all that was left of her.

"Ah, you're back," Susan said.

Her memory place was very like the place she'd hoped to die in.

Agatha sat on the park bench next to her, "I am. I thought it was only fair to offer you one last chance."

Susan laughed. "No, I'm good. It's done now anyway.

"Still Mummy's little soldier?"

Susan reached over to pat her hand, and Agatha stiffened, before relaxing.

"Perhaps my next life will be better."

Agatha smiled, she hadn't expected any different, "I'll make sure of it."

They sat in silence, watching the wind in the trees and listening to the birds and insects.

"You know, you've been my most constant friend," Susan said.

"I can't be your friend, I'm not human."

Susan smiled, "yet whenever things felt the worse, there you were."

"I'd hardly call three times over your lifetime constant."

"Do you remember the first time we met?"

"I do, I even had the idea at the time you were an unusual girl."

«« • »»

Susan was in some kind of dormitory, not exactly sure why, not exactly sure where. She thought she was in a Victorian basement.

The room was small, with filthy walls and floor.

There were six beds in the room, but the scary nurse had closed the creaking door with a solid thud, leaving her all alone.

There were no windows, only two old fashioned fluorescent bar lights hanging from the ceiling.

Which was low and covered with large, dented black painted pipes, suspended from the ceiling with steel ties. Also painted black.

She lay in bed, the covers pulled up high to her neck, fingers tightly linked together under-neath them, looking up at a large dark stain on the ceiling.

It might have been mould or perhaps something worse.

Or maybe it was some kind of supernatural creature.

The closest light was flickering such that it seemed to be slithering across the ceiling.

Susan really wanted to call the nurse, but if anything, she was even more frightening than the thing on the ceiling.

She didn't think it was possible to be any more tense, until the door opened with a screech.

As her heart pounded, Susan thought she might die of fear until a cheery voice called out, "anyone home?"

At which point she got curious, released the choke hold on her fingers and sat up, "I'm home."

A woman was standing in the door way. Or at least Susan assumed it was a woman as she wasn't much more than a female shadow.

"Goodness, look at those lights," the woman said smashing the wall once with the flat or her fist. The light flickered for another few seconds, then shone on brighter than before.

It was an old woman wearing a white dress like a nurse, but different. Though Susan couldn't exactly pinpoint what the difference was.

"Are you all right in here Susan?" she asked.

"I haven't had any supper, is there anything to eat in here?"

"Ah, no, I'm sorry," the old woman said, "you've arrived too late for that, though I could rustle up a cup of tea and some biscuits."

"I would appreciate that," Susan said gravely.

The woman sat down on a chair next to her bed, reached into a shapeless bag Susan hadn't noticed, and pulled out a thermos and a packet of chocolate coated digestives.

She opened the packet and laid them on the bed before Susan, who waited to be invited to take one, while she undid the lid of the thermos and poured the hot tea into it.

She blew a little on it to cool it down before handing it over to Susan. "Please help yourself," she nudged the biscuit packet a little closer.

Susan closed her eyes and bowed her head and said, "For what we are about to receive, may the Lord make us truly thankful. For ever and ever. Amen."

"Amen," the old woman echoed.

Susan took a sip from her tea, then picked one biscuit from the plastic tray.

It looked enormous in her small hand.

Forgetting about the old woman for a mo-ment, she nibbled the biscuit, trying to make it last.

"I like digestives, don't you?" the old woman said.

"Yes, I do too. They help your digestion after dinner you know."

"I'd heard that."

"My name's Susan, what's yours?"

"Agatha."

"That's unusual, what does it mean?"

"Kind, or good."

"That's a good name."

"It used to be Atropos, which means inevitable, but I didn't like that so I changed it."

"I can understand that. But my mother gave me this name, so I'm not sure I could change it."

"She might not mind," said Agatha. "She might think a new name would suit you better now you've grown up."

"That's true. But I can't ask her, she died when I was born."

"How very sad," said Agatha.

"Yes, but I like to think she gave me all that she had. Besides my life I mean.

"I expect she's in heaven looking down on me, and I don't want to disappoint her."

"What if you could have a new Mummy? One who was alive."

Susan thought about it for a long time.

So long that she finished the tea and nibbled another two biscuits down to the crumbs.

"I'd have to say no. I'm not sure she'd like it if I gave up on her just because I hadn't met her."

"I see."

Susan nodded her head emphatically, "it's like that other nurse said, I'm Mummy's little soldier. So I'll soldier on through whatever comes toward me. And I'll battle to become a woman who would make my mother proud."

"It won't be easy."

"Then when it gets hard, I'll swallow my tears and keep marching on."

"Definitely Mummy's little soldier," Agatha dabbed her eyes with a big blue polka-dotted handkerchief.

"I tell you what," she said rummaging in her bag again, "I've got a lovely book to help you through," and she pulled out a small hardback, "it's a sad story about some luckless children," and gave it to Susan.

"Thank you," she said.

"Grow up big and strong," Agatha said as she put the thermos pieces together, and back into the bag, "and make your mother proud.

"Now I must be away, so you keep the biscuits hidden or that nurse will confiscate them."

Susan watched her leave, and only once she was sure Agatha was gone, did she turn the book over and open it up. The first page had her name written in handwriting very much like hers.

She glanced up at the stain, and was relieved to see it was just a stain. As if one of the pipes had burst a long time ago.

《《 • 》》

Susan laughed, "my goodness, what a precocious brat! I wonder you could stand me."

Agatha smiled, "you were so brave that first night in the orphanage, I had to keep track of you as the time passed by."

"I'm not entirely sure I got any better."

"I don't know, it may seem an ordinary life to you, but others found you inspiring."

Susan snorted.

"It's true! Generally, people assume it's their destiny to be happy, healthy and wealthy, but it's people like you who make the most of their lives.

"And you're almost always happier."

Susan smiled, "I suppose I got to almost everything I wanted to."

"Do you remember the second time we met?"

«« • »»

Susan pulled a handkerchief from her pocket, gave the wooden seat a quick flick to clean it, then sat on it to rest.

She tucked her backpack between her legs, took a sip of her take away coffee, and paused to read the graffiti on the chair.

For a so-called elite university, it was disappointingly common.

Jeremy loves Jason, she read.

Frida sucks balls.

Mr Singer is an imperialist.

At this level she'd hoped to find searing critiques of the patriarchy.

Or philosophical positions.

Or just something witty.

Then again, as always, graffiti calls to our most basic needs, so good on Frida.

Always assuming she did indeed suck balls, and the statement wasn't libellous.

And she rather though that perhaps Mr Singer might be a fascist rather than an imperialist.

Unless, of course, he'd travelled here with an Emperor from an alternate universe to overthrow the democratically elected government.

She pulled her favourite soft green cardigan more closely around her.

The gentle breeze was so gentle that most people wouldn't have noticed it, though for Susan it cut deeply through the fine weave.

But, being her first day, she'd wanted to look pretty rather than practical.

There would be plenty of other days to be practical.

Though she was wearing her fine gauge silk Long Johns beneath her blue jeans and a camisole under her t-shirt, and thick woollen socks under her fashionably chunky boots.

The seat she was sitting on was in the quadrangle, which might once have been laid to lawn, but the volume of students passing from building to building had rendered it to dirt and ground up bits of plastic packaging.

She watched the students, hoping a little, someone might take a seat next to her and start talking.

Though she'd planned her charm assault for class.

The quadrangle contained one stunted tree, that received so little light or rain, it was little more than a stick with a leaf on it.

If a bird happened to sit on it, it would collapse under the weight.

Being stunted herself, she felt sorry for the tree, and wanted to set it up with a solar light and automatic sprinkler.

Perhaps it was there as a lesson to the hale and hearty to enjoy their physicality while they could.

She'd heard the original tree, planted when the original, smaller buildings were new, had been struck by lightning.

Perhaps the lesson there was for people like her; enjoy your time while it lasts.

And Susan had every intention of sucking the marrow while she could.

As far as she could go.

Which according to her medical team's predictions, wasn't even long enough to finish university.

Just being there among the young people who hadn't really started living yet, was enough.

In the midst of the scattered, multicoloured groups of chattering students, she felt as though she might live forever.

As though she had all the time in the world.

She looked up and around at the Gothic sandstone building surrounding the quadrangle, trying to orient herself, though the signs were too small for her to read from her seat.

The buildings contained the Library, Arts, Electrical Engineering, and the Wilson Hall; named after Edward Wilson the actor, and used by theatre arts students for live performances.

Her target was Arts, and she gambled the building with the artistic carvings of gargoyles and other creatures was the arts building rather than the library or the theatre.

She couldn't imagine engineering as anything other than the plain one with mullioned win-dows.

She was just getting up when a boy backed into her, knocking her to the ground.

According to the TV shows, he should have immediately turned around to see if she was okay, and then fallen deeply in love with her.

In actuality, he didn't even notice.

She sat on the ground, watching him walk away with his two friends.

That she could not shoot fire from her eyes was surely a miracle, because if she could, those guys would be meat milkshakes splattered across the quadrangle.

She shook her head and started to get up when a hand appeared out of nowhere.

Susan looked up at the owner, a girl with a shaved head, a face full of piercings, and a set of large red headphones.

The girl curled her fingers back into her palm three times, and after a pause did it again.

Only then did Susan realise she was offering a hand up.

Susan reached out towards her, and the girl grabbed her wrist and pulled her up.

"Thanks."

"No worries," the girl said and started walking away.

"Wait," the girl looked back over her shoulder, "what's your name?"

A smile lit up her face, "Grace," she said, and kept walking.

After a moment spent watching her back getting smaller, Susan hefted her backpack, and re-gretfully walked in the direction of the fancy building.

Which turned out to be the library.

Still, the campus bookshop was in the ground floor east, and she needed to see if some of her textbooks had come back into stock.

There was rather a large line of people waiting for attention, but they seemed to be moving along reasonably fast.

She checked her watch and decided she'd wait for ten minutes then try for the Arts building.

As she got nearer the front of the queue, she noticed a strangely familiar old lady working there.

She almost remembered the name, and by the time she's got to the front of the queue she though she had it.

"What can I help you with?" the woman asked.

"Agatha?"

The woman looked at Susan for so long she thought she must have been mistaken.

Then she took a deep breath and said, "how do you know my name."

"On my first day at the orphanage you stopped by my bed with tea and chocolate digestives. And a book."

"So you... recognised me?"

"Yes!"

"That's not possible."

"You didn't stop by my bed?"

"Are you sure it was me?"

"Of course. You haven't aged a day. Literally. Haven't changed at all."

"You shouldn't be able see me. No one sees me as I am."

"Don't you remember me?"

"Of course, you're Mummy's little soldier.'

"That's right," said Susan. "I seem to recall you offered me a new Mummy."

"And I can see you grew up well. Your mother would be pleased you got into a university. Especially this one."

"I did it for you too. Even though Nurse Lambert tried to convince me I'd dreamed you, but I wanted to make you proud. Just in case I met you again."

"What about your first love? Would you change that now?"

Susan smiled, "I haven't met her yet, how could I change her for someone else without giving her a chance?"

Agatha nodded as if it all made sense to her now, "and are you still swallowing your tears?"

Susan looked away, but nodded.

"You'll want to see someone for that. And better sooner than later.

"Now," Agatha slid some books into a paper bag and pulled the handles out, "here are the books you have on hold, and I've slipped in a story about young love. That'll be $34.75."

Susan handed over cash, crumpled her change into the pocket of her jeans, and took the bag.

"Thank you for inspiring me to keep going every day. I hope that next time I see you, I've achieved something remarkable."

"You don't know it, but you already have."

Susan raised the bag in salute, and turned away.

Almost immediately she turned back, but the woman serving the next person wasn't Agatha.

Susan looked around for her, but she was nowhere to be seen.

Checking her watch and realised she was going to be late for class, and ran across the quadrangle to the building with alternating red and yellow bricks, to find it was the arts building.

Up two flights of stairs, the wrong way down the corridor, then back again to room 302.

And the first person she saw when she walked in the door was Grace.

«« • »»

Susan smiled, "ah yes, that day was a big day - meeting you again, then meeting my first love."

"I'm sorry it didn't work out."

"Did you have anything to do with that?"

"Not me, I only do the future. My sister does the present."

Susan turned towards Agatha, "all this time you have a sister and you didn't mention her?"

"Two actually, past and present."

"The past? What does she do?"

Agatha smiled, "weaving mostly. She decides what you remember and what you don't."

"Makes sense. I wish she'd let me forget Grace."

"Too many memories for her to take."

"Do you remember when Grace broke up with me?"

"I'm not sure I could forget that any more than you could."

«« • »»

Susan sat at the bus stop outside the red brick Victorian hospital's main entrance. Hands in her pockets, coat buttoned up to her chin, but she still felt cold.

Colder than normal.

She now knew when she was going to die.

Not the exact date of course, but that she had about three months left.

The road outside the hospital was packed with people coming and going; patients sneaking out for a quick ciggie, visitors arriving with gifts, and discharged patients slowly and carefully walking to cars ready to whisk them back to their normal lives.

Susan didn't see them.

She barely noticed the way the surrounding buildings blocked the wind, trapping the exhaust fumes and noise within the space.

The smell of hospital lingered on her clothes, and as she took a deep, steadying breath she caught notes of antiseptic, coffee, and air-conditioning.

Three months.

She swallowed the tears threatening to rain down her face, then laughed at herself.

Agatha had been right. She should have seen someone for it, and now with twenty years gone by, it was too late.

Though how could an eighteen-year-old know or care about the future.

She, like every other child in a grown-up's body, had assumed she was immortal.

She swallowed again.

And now she knew she wasn't.

There were so many things she'd need to do to get her affairs in order, but today...

She needed a day to eat junk food, drink wine, and snuggle up with Grace to watch horror movies.

To pretend everything was normal.

On which note, where was Grace?

She pulled her phone out of her pocket and saw she had a voice mail.

Hi Susan. It's me.

Look... I, um, I met someone.

And I know you're going through a hard time right now.

But I just can't stand to watch you die.

And by the time you get home I'll be gone.

I've got a new phone so don't try to call me.

We're moving interstate, so don't look for me either.

I, er. I hope you get better.

I.

I.

Take care of yourself.

Susan swallowed.

And listened to the message again.

And again.

And again.

She was about to listen to it one more, when a voice said, "don't. It won't change anything."

She looked up to see Agatha, eyes full of sympathy. Agatha sat down, clasping a shapeless bag in her lap.

"I suppose I should listen to you this time." Her voice wobbled, and she swallowed again."

"You've nothing to lose by letting the tears out now," Agatha said.

A bus paused at the stop, and Agatha waved it on.

"I suppose not, but it's habit now"

They sat in silence, and after a time Agatha waved another bus on.

"So. What do I do now?"

"Well, unless you want to swap lives at this stage, you just carry on."

Susan grinned a little nastily, "should I swap mine for Grace's?"

"If that's what you want."

Susan sighed. "No, I've come this far. And it wouldn't be fair to let a stranger take it the last three months."

"I wish I could tell you it will all be okay, but we both know it won't."

"How could it be when my body is destroying itself. I suppose all those bitter tears have been eating it away all this time."

"Or maybe it's just the cumulation of all those choices you thought were small and didn't matter in the long run."

"Maybe."

Agatha let the silence draw out.

Susan sighed, then swallowed, then laughed.

"I really don't want to do this." She looked up at Agatha, "can't you do something?"

"I offered you a new life. For the third time I might add - most people don't get a single offer."

"No. I mean help with the pain or something."

"That's what the pills in your pocket are for."

"The ones that make me feel ill and sleepy you mean."

Agatha shrugged, "there's no doubt it's a hard choice."

"I should go home, but without Grace..."

Agatha smiled grimly, "I suppose if nothing else she's taken herself off your to do list. And harsh as you might think it, and hard as it may be to do it on your own, you don't have to be brave for her. You can be your own little soldier."

The ghost of a smile flitted across Susan's face as she swallowed, "I suppose you're right about that. I did always try to minimise the impact on her."

"It's funny in a way, that she seemed so strong the first day, but turned out to be so weak," Agatha said.

Susan stiffened, but had to concede that Grace had always been weak. Though she'd made Susan stronger and more capable, shaping her as the protector from life's nastiness.

And it was true that she couldn't be strong for anyone else, let alone herself anymore.

"You wouldn't fancy some ramen with a bucket of saké would you?"

"Ah, as fun as that would be, I have an ap-pointment.

"Another person with an unfortunate fate?"

Agatha laughed, "not this time - family dinner. You've no idea how lucky you are to be alone."

"I always thought family were a source of strength."

"Some families maybe, mine, not so much. Claudia always gets drunk and maudlin, and Laura's always busy fielding phone calls and get-ting texts."

"I guess everyone has their own problems."

"Do what you were planning to do; eat junk food, get shit faced and watch horror movies. To-morrow is plenty of time to write your bucket list."

"I will."

"Ah, I've got a book for you," she rooted around in the bag and handed it to Susan, "it's a story about a ghost that can't let go."

"I appreciate the humour in your choices."

Agatha stood up, "I'll see you again soon."

《《 • 》》

"Did you bring me another book?" Susan asked.

"Not this time. You've passed the need for books."

They sat in silence for a while, then Susan asked, "will it hurt?"

"Not your body, but maybe your mind will re-sist."

"I'm at ease. I had enough time to get every-thing done."

"Well done," said Agatha.

As they watched, a funeral barge approached, and they stood to receive it.

"Will it take long?"

Agatha assessed Susan's fading, wavering form, "you've already begun."

"Any last hints or instructions?"

"I can't follow where you're going."

Susan walked towards the boat and stepped inside it. "Thank you for coming to me. I hope you won't miss me too much."

And with that, the last remains of Susan and the boat dissipated and Agatha was alone.

As Susan's memory collapsed around her, Agatha was ejected back into her body.

She sighed and let Susan's hand go. If only all people were as content with their lives as Susan.

The coins were gone, and she nodded with satisfaction.

She picked up her bag and rummaged around inside for an apple.

No time to rest, it was time for her next client.

THE END

As a small token of my thanks for reading...

Please enjoy 10% off everything (excluding shipping)

at alexandriablaelock.com

with the code moiraiten.

Turn the page for some ideas where to use it,

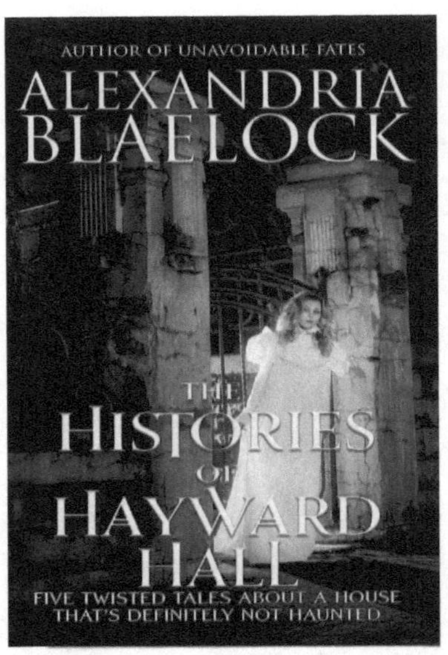

Meet Morag Clementine. The new housekeeper at historic Hayward Hall.

Her practical and capable attitude usually keeps her out of trouble.

bove all, her no-nonsense, get it done approach. And her get in the middle of the scrum outlook. Just as well, because Hayward Hall needs someone like her.

In this genre-spanning collection of original stories, Morag finds herself ensnared in the History of Hayward Hall...

No ordinary housekeeper, can Morag save the house, one century at a time?

All she wants is a place of her own.

When Alison Porter finds a tiny cottage for sale,
she thinks her dreams have come true. Inside virgin
bushland, "Crow Cottage" sits on the smallest parcel of
cleared land.

It's old. It's run down. It's keeping a secret.

Stumbling through a mysterious portal in the garden,
she finds herself in a place of mystery and intrigue. As
the past, present and future collide, she must unravel
the secret, for only then can she reweave the tapestry of
time.

If you love a story of twists and turns, where nothing is
what it seems, grab Weaving the Wildwood today

you go girl!
The opposite
of winning
isn't losing.
it's quitting.
· Martha Rosette Lutz ·
Time for
a nice cup
of tea and
a sit down
Time for
a nice cup
of tea and
a biscuit
there's a book for that

Time for a nice cup of tea and a sit down
BEWARE THE EMPTINESS GREMLINS

ABOUT THE AUTHOR

Australian author Alexandria Blaelock writes mostly fantasy and mystery.

She's appeared in the Stringybark Anthology *Crowd Surfing*, *Pulphouse Fiction Magazine*, and *Ellery Queen's Mystery Magazine*.

She's also written five self-help books applying business techniques to personal matters like getting dressed, tidying up, and feeding friends.

Discover more at https://alexandriablaelock.com.

www.ingramcontent.com/pod-product-compliance
Lightning Source LLC
Chambersburg PA
CBHW030802190726
48285CB00003B/981